ALSO BY JOHN HOULIHAN

The Seraph Chronicles
The Trellborg Monstrosities
The Crystal Void
Tomb of the Aeons
Before The Flood
The Seraph Chronicles Volume One: Tales of the White Witchman

Mon Dieu Cthulhu! The Dubois Escapades
The Crystal Void Illustrated Edition
Feast of the Dead
Shadow of the Serpent
Keeper of the Hidden Flame (coming soon)

OTHER WORKS

Tom or the Peepers' and Voyeurs' Handbook
The Cricket Dictionary
Dark Tales from the Secret War (as editor)
The Constellation of Alarion (science fiction short stories)

The Trellborg Monstrosities is copyright © 2024 John Houlihan

Published by Jolly Big Publishing

All rights reserved.

This edition November 2024

All rights reserved, no reproduction in any form or media without written permission please.

This is a work of fiction, any resemblance to anyone living or dead is entirely coincidental. John Houlihan asserts the moral right to be recognised as the author of the work according to the Copyright Designs and Patents Act 1988.

Any unauthorised use of copyrighted material is illegal. Any trademarked names are used in a historical or fictional manner; no infringement is intended. This is a work of fiction. Any similarity with actual people and events, past or present, is purely coincidental and unintentional except for those people and events described in historical context.

Cover Illustration by Borja Pindado
Design and layout by Tom Hutchings

John Houlihan is a novelist and short story writer publishing books including The Seraph Chronicles and Mon Dieu Cthulhu! series, *The Cricket Dictionary* and the BSFA-award nominated The *Constellation of Alarion*. He has also appeared in numerous sci-fi and fantasy short story collections including Signals, Near Future Fictions, When Shadows Creep, Corridors, Forgotten Sidekicks, Musketeers vs Cthulhu and many more.

He currently works for Modiphius Entertainment as an ENNIE-award winning game designer, creative lead and narrative director and works for many other TTRPG companies including Wizards of the Coast, Need Games and Monolith. He was also editor-in-chief of *Dragon+*. Before that he was a journalist and broadcaster for over thirty years, working in news, sport and especially videogames. He worked for *The Times*, *Sunday Times* and *Cricinfo* and is the former editor-in-chief of *Computer and Video Games.com*. He still works as a video game consultant and script writer.

Away from the written word he has an unnatural fondness for cricket, football, snowboarding, cycling, music, playing guitar and all forms of sci-fi, fantasy and horror. He has an unnatural dread about writing about himself in the third person and currently lives in his home town of Watford in the UK, because, well frankly, someone has to.

Find him at www.john-houlihan.net and @johnh259 on X.com

CONTENTS

THE SERAPH CHRONICLES BOOK ONE:

THE TRELLBORG MONSTROSITIES

CHAPTER ONE:
DIPPING A TOE

"Six of us came out, now I alone remain and it shan't be long before this bitter cold claims me too. I will be glad, for even if by some chance these wounds aren't the death of me, after the things I have witnessed tonight, I'm not sure I wish to live anymore.

It began as it had many times before on a moonlit night in early '43. Four stalwart lads of the Section and I, plus our rather unsettling guest, pushed off from the deck of the submarine HMS Uredd launching our three fragile canvas canoes Badger, Fox, and Otter into the rolling swells of the Norwegian Sea.

Our destination was clear enough, a small village called Trellborg, some forty miles east of Tromso on the Norwegian-Finnish border, but our mission was an altogether murkier affair. Even though the briefing had been relatively straightforward, our objective most certainly was not. 'Escort Mister Seraph to a rendezvous with the Norwegian resistance and en route render him every assistance possible' is a definitive, but hardly enlightening set of orders. When I raised it with the brigadier, he merely shrugged, confided 'mum's the word' and indicated that I would get nothing more.

I'm a bluff, plain speaking kind of cove myself, but from the very beginning I was uneasy about our mysterious Mister Seraph. Not only was he apparently a civilian with little training, which meant we'd have to nursemaid him through hostile territory, but something about his otherworldly manner, long, almost unnaturally white hair and penetrating eyes was distinctly unnerving. He wasn't much to look at considering, being pale, thin and dressed in an eccentric mix of military and civilian clobber topped off by a long, rather shabby looking cloak. His fey, cryptic responses grated almost instantly and I felt this might be a very long mission indeed. Still, orders were orders and they came from the very top which meant we had no choice in the matter. I took little comfort from the Brigadier's reassurance that, 'Mister Seraph is most assuredly on the side of the angels.'

Our paddles bit into the waves as behind us the Uredd slunk below the surface and with the moon playing peek-a-boo with the clouds, we were soon approaching the enemy-held coastline. The gods were kind that night and although fearsomely cold, the sea was as tranquil as I have ever seen her, as we slowly reduced the distance to the main entrance to the fjord.

The Uredd had dropped us off in relatively sheltered waters between the mountainous isles of Vannra and Arnøya, about as close as could reasonably be managed with any safety, but even then we had little intelligence on enemy marine concentrations in the area. There could be anything waiting for us out there. We had a long hard slog ahead of us until we reached the relative safety of dry land and we'd have to do it before dawn crept across this bleak part of the world and caught us exposed on the open water.

Ahead, Fox and Otter under Sergeant Jones and Corporal Bennett were making good time and I glanced quickly behind me to see how Seraph was faring. But he seemed to be matching me stroke for stroke with perfect timing and he gave a curt nod to acknowledge my unasked question. Perhaps I'd underestimated the man? We paddled on in silence.

For the first couple of hours, everything went better than could be expected and our canoes pierced the icy waters with barely a murmur. Ice floes and small bergs gleamed in the sporadic moonlight and in that vast empty water, surrounded by snow capped peaks, we could have been paddling towards the very end of the world. We were almost at the mouth of the great Lynengen Fjord, when Bennett's hushed voice drifted across the water in the prearranged signal, I followed his gaze to the east where about two miles away, a German cruiser had emerged, steaming its way through a channel into the sound.

If it held course it would be upon us and soon and I tried to remain calm and think rationally. If we paddled hard, we might just make it to the far shore and shelter in the wooded tributaries beneath that mountainous dormant volcano. But the cruiser was approaching fast and it would be a close run thing, I was just about to issue the order when Seraph whispered, "Major Powell?"

"What is it, Seraph? I'm rather busy here."

"Major Powell, with respect, we will never make that shore in time, but there are other, nearer means of concealment. Look to those ice floes. With speed we should be able to conceal ourselves amongst them."

"How the devil...?" but I stifled my question, immediately seeing he was right, confound him, and I barked the orders. Urgency lent us speed and we paddled furiously, our blades slicing through the water until all three canoes were nestling in the lee of the protective ice. The droning of the cruiser's engines came ever closer and its searchlights swept out across the water, piercing the darkness.

We hunkered down, trusting that our camouflage would conceal us, but in spite of the cold, I could feel beads of sweat break out on my back. There was a moment when one of the beams seemed to catch us full on and I awaited the awful shout of discovery, but then it swept past and was gone. The engine note changed as she came about and turned, heading north in search of other prey, funnels belching plumes of black smoke.

As the cruiser steamed away there were grins and thumbs up from the men and I breathed out a breath I didn't know I had held.

"Nice work, Seraph."

"My pleasure, Major, but you shouldn't sound so surprised. We are on the same side after all."

I nodded, conceding his point and we fell to it again. For the next couple of hours we hugged the coastline of the desolate western shore, keeping our distance from the lights of isolated houses and villages on the eastern side. The water was placid as we moved inland and the snow-tipped mountains of the Lynengen Alps seemed tranquil as we journeyed up the ever-narrowing channel.

Soon we were rounding the deserted isle of Arnøya and looking south east to the entrance of the great Lynengen fjord. We'd been going for a few hours then and I signalled the men to heave to and take a rest in the shallows, while I surveyed the way ahead. Through field glasses I could see the distant lights of the small hamlet of Olderhalden on the eastern shore and once we were past that, we should have a clear run down the lesser fjord and the rendezvous point. The limited intelligence we did have said there was a small German garrison stationed there and we'd need to slip past it to progress.

The men busily tucked into their rations and I prised open a Type E and offered some to Seraph, who declined.

"So Seraph, before we make our final approach, perhaps you'd care to share with me the reason we're taking this little midnight paddle through the fjords?"

"I'm afraid I must humbly decline, Major... for the moment. Even now, if you or your men were taken, it could compromise certain assets we have here in Norway. When we are closer, I will be able to share more."

"Not very satisfactory, old boy. If I'm risking my men's lives and my..."

"No need to explain, I too would naturally wish to know more in your position. All I can tell you is that if what I suspect is true, our mission may prove pivotal to the war effort. But I'm afraid I must leave it at that."

"Very well, can't blame a man for trying," I harrumphed.

"No, Major, I cannot." His answers were so measured, so reasonable, that despite any qualms, I digested them and the rest of my ration in silence.

Twenty minutes later found us threading the needle across the mouth of the lesser fjord. My binoculars had revealed a sparsely populated hamlet, but we soon found out why the Germans hadn't defended it in any depth. A damn great chain had been stretched across the water to protect the channel and we'd have to negotiate it under the view of two watchtowers on either shore. Fortunately the obstacle was designed to block larger vessels than us, but it would still be damn ticklish to pass through unobserved. I drew the men together and outlined the plan and told Barker and Mitchell to unpack their rifles. If those watchtowers came to life, I wanted the search lights shot out before they could spot us, then we'd have to paddle for our very lives.

But as we approached the chain, all was going as well as could be hoped. The moon was shrouded in cloud and the night was once again darker than Hitler's heart. We'd spread out into a line abreast formation with Fox and Otter flanking us on either side and painstakingly we made it to the chain unobserved. In the village, the headlights of a motorbike starting up, caused a momentary flutter, but then it revved up, drove off up the coast and once again all was silent. I risked another quick look at the towers, but there was no movement atop either one. A hearty heave with the paddle was sufficient to depress the chain for our shallow draft to pass over and then I watched Bennett and Barker's canoe repeat the manoeuvre. Still nothing, then while Mitchell covered the tower Jones inched the canoe forward, but whether it was a stray wave or the chain came up too early, the canoe suddenly shuddered and Mitchell overbalanced, plunging into the icy waters with a splash. Immediately all my senses came alert, was that a voice from the watchtower? Jones was over now, but where was Mitchell?

Quickly I signalled Corporal Bennett to push on and half turned the canoe about, looking for Mitchell to surface. But nothing disturbed the water. Damn, the man could swim like an eel, where was he? The moments ticked by, without any relief and now the moon began to threaten to emerge from the clouds, making it dangerous to linger. Quickly, I scanned the watchtowers, nothing. Where was Mitchell? Damn. we couldn't wait, couldn't afford the risk of discovery. I felt a hand on my shoulder and a voice whispered, "He is lost Major."

"And how could you possibly know that?"

"I can't explain, but he is. We must go now."

I turned, blazing with anger, ready to crucify the man, but Seraph's gaze was calm, even, and I saw only truth there. My rage dissipated and just at that moment there was movement from one of the watchtowers and so with a last scan of the water, I reluctantly signalled Bennett and we slipped off into the protective folds of the night.

The first fingers of dawn were beginning to light the east when we pulled in and took the next opportunity to rest. Three hours of hard paddling had brought us deep inland, past the steep mountains and flowing waters of the fjord and the men were dog tired, so we secreted ourselves in a small tributary near the rendezvous point, unloaded the canoes and buried them under the snow.

I lit a ruminative pipe and stared out across the water. Casualties are a fact of war, but it doesn't make it any damned easier when you lose a man on an operation. One just has to try and put it out of one's mind and concentrate on the job in hand.

Bennett and Jones organised some chow while Seraph sat a little apart on a rock, seemingly alone with his thoughts. Maybe now would be the time to discover a little more about why we were actually here? I went across and by way of introduction offered him the pouch.

"Thank you, Major, but no."

"Hm, filthy habit I know." I sat down next to him. "My apologies about my strong words at the chain. He was a good man."

"I understand, Major, his sacrifice will be remembered."

"Well, let's make sure it counts. Now, Seraph, are you ready to tell me more about this mission of ours?"

"I would Major, but I think we might have some other, more pressing business at hand." He nodded, indicating the band of armed figures that had suddenly appeared to cover us from the nearby heights. They had us cold, but even so, I made to grab for my Sten. Seraph's hand stayed me in a surprisingly powerful grip and he called out, *Hilsener!*"

"*Hilsener, Britisk…*" there followed a babble of what I knew must be Norwegian.

"He says hello and keep your hands away from your weapons, Major. We don't want any accidents."

"You know them?" I blurted.

"Of them. These are the men of the local resistance Major, the ones sent to meet us. Now let's play nice and go parley shall we?"

Half an hour later, we were hunkered down in the remote hunting lodge which was to have been our rendezvous and served as the Norwegians' part-time base. They were a small group, hunters and farmers mainly from this rather remote region, but fiercely patriotic, real salts of the earth. They shared tobacco and pickled herring with our men and they were led by a grizzled, bearded cove called Sven, who spoke harsh, accented English and took great delight in recounting the havoc they had inflicted on the occupying forces.

"But that is not vy we haf called on you Mister Seraph. Germans we can handle, it is this bis-i-ness at Trellborg." At the name several his men muttered darkly and one crossed himself. "*Der Finsk*, the Finns have always been a law unto themselves, peculiar, you know, but good fighters. Sometimes we shelter just over the border there, after we have attacked German convoys on the highway. We are allies, brothers even." He stopped and lit his pipe.

"But lately? Ach, we hear nothing. A month ago, SS with a strange badge came in big convoy, occupied the village, cut it off. How can they do this you ask? Pfaw, this is many miles from civilisation, who is to know? The snow knows no borders and the *Finsk* fear the Russians as much as the Germans. Yet this…" He paused and breathed out another great gout of smoke and stared into the flames.

"Go on," said Seraph.

"This is something different. I am a practical man, Mister Seraph, not one prone to superstition. But there is something… strange going on there. Olaf, my brother, was in the village with his woman when they came. He called us few times on hidden radio, told us of the occupation, how they build camp outside village, make expedition onto mountain. Soon there are unusual noises, strange mists, weird lights come from there. Villagers are terrified, won't go out at night. We listen for few days, but then radio goes quiet."

"How many SS?"

"A platoon, maybe fifty men, plus many prisoners, slaves."

"And this insignia? Their badge?"

"Olaf says it looks like sun, black sun with lightning flashes." Seraph nodded softly and muttered something inaudible.

"Did he mention their commander at all?"

"Yes, small man, one-eyed, he had eyepatch and the other…"

"Fiery?"

"Hm, yes, how you say burns like coals, yes? Even SS seem to fear him."

"Thank you Sven, this has been most useful."

"So, what will you do with this information, *Britisk*?"

"Do? Oh, we'll take a stroll over to Trellborg and see for ourselves of course."

CHAPTER TWO: TROLL COUNTRY

The next morning found us fed and rested and heading out onto the snow on borrowed skis. The Norwegians assured us we were too remote to attract any German attention, so I let the men off the leash for the night for god knows when – or indeed if – we would have the chance again. The rest of the evening was spent with the partisans sharing strong language and stronger spirits with Sven delighting in relating some of the more unusual and macabre punishments they'd inflicted on the occupying forces.

Seraph sat in a corner staring into the fire, the closest I ever saw those placid features come to brooding and despite my entreaties, he would not entertain any questions until we had passed what he called, 'the point of no return.' Yet something of what he had heard gave that most imperturbable of men pause for thought, that was plain indeed.

We moved through the frozen landscape like wraiths, Sven acting as our guide while the rest of the partisans melted away back to their everyday lives. Even for men in prime condition, cross-country skiing is a strenuous affair and I exhaled great cones of breath and could feel my pulse quicken in my forehead as we traversed snow-choked forest and pushed up hill and mercifully, down dale. Sven was always waiting for us just short of the next ridge or hilltop, spying out the land on the other side and it was a hard morning's work before we came to our first major objective and our first major obstacle.

Only one obstruction lay between us and Trellborg, the arterial road which leads to Tromso. Sven had assured us that even in broad daylight the crossing should be relatively easy, but what he hadn't counted on was what looked like a half an armoured German division parked up in front of us apparently stopped to admire the scenery.

"Damn, this I was not expecting," said Sven as he, Seraph and I perched on the lip of the ridge overlooking the road.

"Can we go around?"

"Not very easily, Major, but this is the only gap for twenty kilometres. It would mean a long detour."

"So we wait for darkness, sneak through."

"We could Major, but speed is now of the essence," said Seraph.

"What then? You're not suggesting that we simply waltz through there in broad daylight are you?"

"In broad daylight, no, but hm… can you feel that breeze? I have a feeling that conditions may be about to change. Stay here."

"Breeze?" I muttered, but the forest was utterly still with nary a breath stirring the leaves. "What the hell are you talking about man?" But Seraph was already down the slope and had struck out into the trees. Content to leave him to it, whatever it was, we continued to observe the convoy. But those Germans weren't going anywhere soon and I began to calculate how and where we might best slip through them once night came down.

Lost in tactical thought, I didn't notice the creeping chill at first and only became aware of the change when Sven nudged me and pointed. Despite the bright winter sun overhead, a bank of misty fog was quickly rolling in along the valley road where the German convoy was strung out, borne on a wind from the east which seemed to penetrate our very bones. Faintly, or perhaps I imagined it, it seemed to carry a voice chanting in a language that was strange yet familiar. Perhaps it was just a trick of the wind distorting some German's call?

For they were astir now, rushing back into their vehicles and huddling inside to escape the piercing frost with a flurry of curses. We watched as the mist enfolded them and where minutes before, the convoy had stood out clear as day, now it was wrapped in a shroud of dim shapes and outlines. Quickly, I signalled to the men to make ready, for we could not pass up such an opportunity however strange the phenomenon seemed. It was only then that I noticed Seraph had rejoined us.

"Ah, Seraph, it seems our problem is solved."

"Indeed, how convenient."

"Too damned convenient, but I'm not going to ask how or why, just be grateful and take it. Make ready to cross and not a sound mind." Sven said nothing, but gave Seraph a long, evaluative stare.

"It seems the old gods favour us today Mister Seraph."

"It seems they do Sven, it seems they do."

The passage across the road was as tense an affair as I have ever experienced. Despite the supreme chill of the fog, I could feel my pulse hammering in my throat as our shadows silently glided down the snow bank and onto the black ice of the road. Ghosting between the bulky armoured shapes of two panzers, we moved in single file, carrying our skis over our shoulders, hastening to be gone from that place. Discovery would mean death, but our luck held and Sven and the men were through and disappearing into the fringes of the forest on the other side when the command rang out. Just Seraph and I remained on the verge of the road.

"Halt! Who goes there?" rang out in German and dimly I could see a head under a *Stahlhelm* peering out of a turret hatch. Quietly, I drew my Webley.

"It's Churchill and Stalin," answered Seraph in perfect German. "We decided to come for the fishing." Sniggers from inside the turret greeted this witticism.

"Quite the comedian, aren't we?"

"Ach, relax, we're just going for a piss."

"Well, I hope you freeze your balls off." The turret hatch shut with a clang and I eased my pistol back into its holster with some difficulty, my hand shaking. Seraph gave me a smile, a quick nod, and in an instant we were under the safety of the trees. Pushing hard, we followed the others' tracks to where they had spread out across a ridge, covering our retreat with Stens at the ready. We were not an instant too soon either, for already I could see the fog begin to dissipate, wisps and curls unravelling, revealing the armoured bulk of the convoy again, the first sentries re-emerging. Gratefully, we dropped behind the brow of the ridge, affixed our skis again and pushed on into the depths of the interior.

The rest of the day passed slowly as we skied through a realm of isolated peaks and old, still forest where it seemed human feet might not have passed in a thousand years. 'Troll country' Sven called it and I think he was only half joking. The snow was not heavy or deep as we inched toward the border, but it sapped the will and the legs and by the time the light was fading and we were wearily settling into our retreat in another remote hunter's lodge, I was as tired as I'd ever felt. It had been a long day, but Sven soon had a fire roaring in the grate and as dusk fell, we set to on our ration packs greedily, hot, washing them down with hot, sweet tea and chocolate to restore our lost energy.

I set the sentry duty and as the first wolves' howls began to pierce the dark, I joined Sven and Seraph a little apart from the men on one side of the fire. Sven smoked in that stolid imperturbable way the Norwegians have and I lit a sympathetic pipe and addressed the mysterious Seraph.

"Well then Seraph, I believe we may have passed a tipping point and the time has come for you to spill the beans." To my surprise Seraph nodded.

"I dare say, Major, and first my apologies for having kept you in the dark so long. On some matters this must remain the case, but you deserve to know more about this mission and you shall know as much as I can tell you. About a month ago my department received some very unusual intelligence."

"And that department is…?"

"Well, its sobriquet is not widely known, but you can call it Department E. We deal with some of the more… let us just say curious scenarios this war has thrown up."

"Go on."

"It is not widely known outside certain circles, but the Nazi's beloved leader der Führer has a fervent belief in the occult, a belief which has grown as the war has gone on and his reverses have mounted."

"I see."

"Your scepticism does you credit Major, but believe me it is very real. The SS that Sven mentioned are not really SS at all, but part of the Black Sun brigade, a special unit formed to seek out certain esoteric artefacts which Hitler believes could turn the tide against the Allies. These particular villains are led by a very dangerous man, Ludwig von Obertorff, a Nazi scientist, occultist and member of the Thule Society. He must believe that one such object lies near Trellborg."

"Preposterous, I've never heard anything like it. You mean we're risking our lives because of Hitler's superstitions?!"

"A little more quietly if you will, Major, your men are listening." Sven interjected.

"You don't mean you believe this nonsense?" I hissed.

"What I believe or disbelieve does not matter, what matters is what is. Yet I am surprised you do not believe the evidence of your own eyes."

"What do you mean?"

"The path through the convoy, ze mist, that vos no happy accident if I am not mistaken, Mister Seraph?" said Sven and to my astonishment Seraph nodded.

"Bullets and tanks are not the only weapons we employ to oppose evil, Major," he said. "You should remember that as this mission goes on, for things are bound to become stranger. If von Obertorff is involved, this must be something important, something significant. He doesn't come out to play for anything less. Can you shed any more light on the matter, Sven?"

"Not speziffically, but up here in the far north the old gods are not quite such a distant outlandish superstition. There are stories, handed down through the generations and who knows what is true and what is legend? But there are sites said to be sacred to the old Viking gods and near Trellborg there is one of them. Perhaps that is what they seek?"

"Do you know which god?" asked Seraph intently.

"The hanged god, Mister Seraph, the hanged god."

Seraph must have seen my look of puzzlement. "He means Odin, Major."

After that Sven lit another pipe and fell silent, and Seraph fell into a reverie watching the flames flicker in the grate. I retired outside to see to the sentries, then smoke a pipe in the cold night air and mull over his strange words. All this talk of ancient gods, unnatural artefacts, and Nazi occultism was unsettling. Give me a clean fight and a tangible enemy any day rather than this errant mumbo jumbo. Yet Seraph's earnestness and Sven's conviction was unsettling and once I'd gone back inside and bedded down, I fell into a restless sleep.

I had seen many dark things during the four years of this hellish war, brutal close combat, senseless cold-hearted murder, comrades and friends taken before my very eyes, but that night my dreams were peopled by stranger terrors, white creatures in the snow, a strange one-eyed wayfarer and something, a shape, a weapon, blazing bright, in a halo of searing light. I seemed to see Mitchell's eyes peering up from beneath the freezing water, his lips moving, soundlessly mouthing something. I was unable to move and there was a horrid low chanting, like the moaning ecstasy of demons and a weird, unnatural ceremony was coming to a ghastly conclusion. A hand reached out, something, someone had hold of me, was grabbing me, a bony hand was on my shoulder. Suddenly wide awake, I made to scream but a hand was over my mouth, choking off any sound. Then my revolver was in hand, the barrel of the Webley pointing directly at the space between Seraph's eyes.

"Gently Major, I bruise easily. Time to get up."

"What? What the…?"

"You were dreaming. A German patrol is on the way, it'll be here soon. I imagine you'll want to prepare a welcome?" he smiled.

"How, how do… how can you know?" I stammered struggling to sit up.

"I don't sleep much, Major, and I always like to know where my enemy is."

"But the sentry…?"

"Won't have seen them, but trust me the Germans are working their way up the valley as we speak. They will be here in less than fifteen minutes. You can take that as gospel."

I glared at him for a moment, ready to argue, but one look at that face was enough to tell me it was useless. Even if he was wrong, I couldn't take the chance and somehow, infuriatingly, I knew he was right. Outside, the first streaks of dawn were breaking as I hurried to rouse the men.

Their leader, a Hauptmann from his insignia, was a decent soldier or perhaps the resistance had simply schooled them well. Even though we were deep inside German-held territory the ten-man patrol approached the cabin cautiously and in good order, with scouts sniffing the way ahead and investigating the building thoroughly before waving their comrades forward. They were *Gebirgskorps Norwegen*, German mountain corps by the look of them, tough, experienced troops who carried themselves bravely in their white winter camouflage and edelweiss insignia.

With their objective apparently free and unoccupied, their leader ordered them to stand easy and like soldiers the world over they immediately doubled at the slouch, chatting, smoking, telling smutty jokes, and breaking out a portable stove to brew up coffee in the open air. The Hauptmann disappeared inside with his NCO, while the radio man broke out his set, presumably to make contact with their base.

From where we were secreted, some way back from the cabin in the small bluffs that surround it, I exhaled a silent sigh of relief. Even though we had them well covered, this was one engagement I was keen to avoid. Their stance suggested nothing more than a routine patrol and they didn't seem to be looking for anything or anyone in particular. I was quite happy to give up our temporary home until they packed up and went on their way and it seemed thanks to Seraph's warning that we might just get away with avoiding a fight. We weren't here to take on the regular German army, let alone elite units like these mountain men. It's an old maxim, but sometimes the best ambush is the one you don't actually have to actually spring.

Seraph lay three yards away from me, eyes closed as if he were in a deep sleep or perhaps a deeper meditation. Even though he was unarmed, he'd refused the offer of my revolver, claiming he had no use for such weapons. Sven lay on my other side, quiet but watchful, cradling his hunting rifle and I'd deployed Jones with the Bren to the North, while Bennett and Barker covered from the east with their silenced Stens. Minutes passed, the Germans drank their coffee and there was the occasional wail of chatter from the radio as the operator dialled through the frequencies.

Eventually, after about ten minutes, the Hauptmann and his NCO re-appeared from inside and like any good officer he gave them the hurry up, ordering his troops to fall in double smartish and make ready to depart. While the sergeant harangued them none too gently, the Hauptman lit himself a solitary cigarette and perched on the wood pile to watch their preparations. Soon they'd be on their way and I was hoping that they'd head west, so that they would be going in exactly the opposite direction to us when we set off.

"Your revolver, Major?" Seraph's urgent whisper caught me off guard.

"They're about to leave, I'm really not sure it's nece—"

"I need that revolver Major, now if you please. Herr Hauptmann has just discovered us."

"What? I mean how?" I hissed, hastily undoing my holster and handing him the heavy Webley.

"No time, Major, just be ready." I looked at Sven who gave a nod.

I glanced at the Hauptmann again, he had let the cigarette drop from his hand and it had fallen into the snow. I could almost see the thought cross his brow and his mouth opened and he managed to utter "Achtu…" before Sven's rifle bullet took him through the throat. Then I was opening up with my Sten and I could hear the steady muffled thud thud of the other suppressed Stens and the short staccato bursts of the Bren and louder shots as Seraph fired the revolver beside me. It must have taken moments, but it seemed to last an eternity and I was automatically ramming in another magazine and making ready to fire again, but there was nothing left to fire at. They had been right under our guns and they had died to man, hardly even managing to get a shot off in return. The coffee pot still bubbled on the lit stove.

It was a short, bloody, brutal encounter and even though these were enemy soldiers, I felt a certain sympathy for these men who we had gunned down so casually. Yet were it not for Seraph's uncanny presci-ence, the positions could so easily have been reversed and it might have been us that ended our lives knifed in the back, shot in our beds, or lying there leaking our life's blood out into the snow. I bent over the officer, his lifeless eyes staring straight up into the sky. "Sergeant Jones."

"Sah?"

"Search them thoroughly, conceal the bodies, and then sweep the area clean. Remove any trace that we were ever here."

"Sah."

As I rifled through the officer's map case, Seraph came over and joined me, holding out the revolver grip first. "Thank you, Seraph, decided to take part in the slaughter after all?"

"Not exactly Major, in this case my particular target was the radio." He indicated the set which was cracked and smashed by several .455 calibre shaped holes drilled through its case. "Von Obertorff must have no word of our coming."

"How did you know that the Hauptmann had discovered us?"

"Oh, I have an instinct for these matters, but in this case it was simple observation. You left your slipper of British tobacco on the porch, Major." He handed me the pouch, "Herr Hauptmann could hardly miss it when he came out."

Damn him, he was right.

Another half a morning's hard march and ski had brought us to the ridge overlooking the hamlet of Trellborg. I had brooded and fumed most of the way, angry with myself for a foolish mistake which had not only cost the lives of the German patrol, but more importantly risked our mission itself. I was angry with Seraph too, unreasonably so, for not only did he refuse to make a song and dance about it, but continued to behave with that kind of calm equanimity that was more infuriating than the reproachful lecture he would have been fully entitled to deliver.

As we had crossed a low featureless plane, Sven had skied up alongside me to inform me that we were just crossing the Norwegian-Finnish border. I remarked somewhat flippantly that I would have expected some kind of reception so that we could present our papers.

"The snow knows no boundary lines Major, neither does our friend Mister Seraph."

"What do you mean?"

"Ach. come, even an old hound such as I can see there may be difficulties, when there are two top dogs in the pack."

"I don't know what you mean, sir." I said and it sounded rather pompous even to my own ears.

"Come now, Major, Mister Seraph is I vould say is an extraordinary individual. We have a word in old Norse, *seiðr*, a wielder of the magic of the old gods. I believe Mister Seraph may be such a one, a seer or vizard as you say, able to command unnatural forces on our behalf. If even half of what he suggests is true, we may need more than mere bullets alone to defeat these Nazis."

"I've never heard anything so…"

"Major, do not dismiss my vords so lightly or place your beliefs in what you think you know. Up here in the far frozen reaches of the vorld, the normal laws and boundaries of civilisation no longer apply. I am no credulous naïf, believe me, but I have seen strange things, vyrdling things that no rational words or mind could explain. If we have one who could help us combat such dark powers, then perhaps you should vork with him, not against him. That is all I have to say."

"Perhaps you're right, Sven, perhaps you are." He nodded.

"Good, I am glad to hear it, now ve must hurry for it seems the Germans have eyes everywhere, even here, in the middle of nowhere." He pointed to a distant black dot in the surly skies. The drone of the reconnaissance plane's engine began to reach us.

"Make for the trees, make for the trees!" I ordered and we skied hard. We watched under their protective shelter as a small plane, a Fieseler Storch, passed us by, and then banked before disappearing off to the west.

CHAPTER THREE: THE HOUNDS OF TRELLBORG

Two hours further on and we finally found ourselves secreted above the hamlet of Trellborg and Seraph, Sven, and I had drawn a little way ahead of the men to spy out the lay of the land. My binoculars swept up and down the small collection of wooden cabins or *mökki* along Trellborg's main thoroughfare for the umpteenth time, but there was still no sign of movement.

"What do you make of it, Seraph?" He was silent for a moment, then emerged from underneath the cloak where apparently he had been meditating.

"Strange, I detect almost nothing, but…"

"Vot is it?" Sven asked.

"No, I thought there was something, but it's too faint, like an after-image."

"Perhaps we should go down and investigate?" I suggested, "It appears we have little to fear and much to learn."

"An excellent idea, Major, but let's be cautious, something here doesn't feel quite right."

"No smoke from the fires and even the birds are silent. Vere have all the people gone?"

"Exactly Sven, where indeed?" Seraph let the question hang.

I quickly briefed the men to spread out and search the village, but detailed Barker, a hulking young brute of a Scotsman and a fine shot to boot to provide overwatch with the Bren. If we got caught with our pants down in the village, I wanted someone covering what would no doubt be a messy retreat.

We crept into the hamlet like wisps of falling snow and it was quiet, tense, as if the surrounding woods themselves were straining to hear our every step. Sven took the lead, picking his way carefully from tree to tree and then positioned himself outside the first door, while Jones and Bennett flanked him. Using the barrel of his hunting rifle to tease it open, Sven suddenly ducked inside and there was silence for a moment then a fierce Norwegian oath.

The two lads from the Section piled in after him and I cocked my Sten ready to fire off a burst if anything untoward emerged.

"Easy Major, I don't believe we're in any danger right now." For once I was glad of Seraph's calm assertion and I even lowered my weapon slightly. Sure enough, moments later Bennett ducked his head around the door post and said, "You'd best come see this, sir."

Inside, the one room cabin seemed unremarkable, small but tidily furnished and intimately cosy in the way of those who have to endure in the coldest of climes. Skins and furs adorned the walls but the bed and tables were covered in the warm, colourful fabrics so beloved of the Finns and there were all the usual accoutrements and minutiae of a family life. But the smell, by gods, something was rotten in the state of Denmark and it pervaded the confined space. Sven wasn't long in pointing out the source either, a cooking pot hanging over the stove.

"Ach, ze fish stew, it has gone rotten and smells like Eva Brown's pussy." His coarse jest broke the tension and suddenly we were all grinning, even the otherworldly Seraph, but his next pronouncement took a more sombre turn. "Ach, it has been left for a day more and look, the fire has just been allowed to burn out. This is not like the Finns. Here the flame is life itself."

"Does that mean they left suddenly?" I asked.

"Ja, left or vere taken."

"How many villagers lived here, Sven?" enquired a thoughtful Seraph.

"Hm, tventy, maybe tventy five with the children. A small community."

"What shall we do now?"

"Let's keep looking," said Seraph

Outside, I signalled to Barker that we were heading deeper into the village and got a thumbs up by way of acknowledgment. We spread out this time and worked our way through the remaining cabins, but in every one, the picture was pretty much the same. There was no sign of disturbance, but it seemed as if the inhabitants had got up and left in the middle of some everyday task, or simply been spirited away. It was more than a little eerie. One or two called away on an errand, you might expect, but a whole village at once? Something very dark had happened here or I was no judge, and I suppressed an involuntary shiver. I was just about to leave the third cabin of my search, when I noticed that unusually it seemed to have a back door. Curiosity piqued, I opened it hesitantly and peered inside.

"Good God!" My cry must have been louder than I imagined, for it brought Sven and the others running. The door led directly outside into the cold and a small corral full of wooden kennels which was shielded from the interior side of the village. What had drawn my exclamation was a most disturbing discovery, for it was the village dogs, one of those ubiquitous packs which inhabit every small hamlet in the north and live and work alongside their human masters, helping them survive in this harshest of climes. Yet these canines were still and lifeless, as if they had been flash frozen in an instant.

And their bearing! My god, the pack had been caught mid charge and leaping for they were snarling and barking, fangs bared, hair stood on end, eyes wide with aggression or terror – as if they were facing some dreadful mortal enemy. It was a most chilling and sinister scene, far more affecting than discovering them shot or torn to pieces by some natural enemy.

"Ach, these are of Sptizes and Karelians, bear hunters. How did this happen to them?" Sven articulated what we all were thinking and naturally enough everyone seemed to turn to Seraph for an explanation. But he seemed not to see us and was already amongst the still forms, examining them from different angles, bending over, pausing and even sniffing them.

"I'm not sure." Seraph's fingertips brushed one of the dogs' heads and in a moment its entire body crumbled into a fine powder which blended into the snow.

I believe it was that singular moment, watching that poor mutt disintegrate which persuaded me of the reality and magnitude of the supernatural threat we faced. Up until that time, my stodgy rational mind had been able to dismiss Seraph's witchery as mere superstition and folklore, but the sight of those frozen hounds disturbed me more deeply than I can articulate. They say we British are more sentimental about our dogs than our women and perhaps they're right, for in that moment I started to comprehend that the enemy we faced must be more than merely mortal. Still, it wouldn't do to show such fear in front of the men. I could see in their faces, hardened veterans though they were, that this abhorrent little tableaux had spooked them deeply.

"Very well, Seraph, continue your investigation here. Bennett, Jones, finish searching the village. Stay together and if you see so much as a twig out of place, shoot it."

"Sir." The pair of them trotted off, clearly relieved to have escaped the sinister scene.

"A bad bizness, Mister Seraph, vot on earth could have done this?"

"Nothing on earth I suspect, Sven."

"What then? How do you explain this, Seraph?"

"I can't Major, but clearly some extraordinary agency has been at work here. The dogs frozen, the village picked clean of people with no sign of any struggle. What did this I can only begin to guess at, but one thing I do know, von Obertorff is behind it, that I would bet my last farthing on."

"But why did he take them?"

"For no good purpose I'll wager. The most powerful magics demand a heavy toll, a ritual sacrifice sometimes blood, sometimes lives, sometimes both."

Sven spat. "Pff, then ve must find them, kill him, and rescue these souls before he succeeds in vatever his fell purpose is."

"Amen to that, Sven," said Seraph. "Amen to that."

"Major, Major! Come quickly, we've found someone, a live one!" Bennett's voice echoed across the village and hurling caution to the wind, we leapt over walls of the corral and hot footed it to the last cabin on the other side. Jones was inside, helping lay out a big, blond man on the bed. He was dirty and dishevelled and appeared to be sorely wounded, a bloody trail crossed the floor.

"He must have heard our voices sir and crawled up out from that trap door under the bed," explained Bennett.

"He's pretty badly hurt, sir, but let me try and patch him up," added Jones as he laid on with the medical kit, while the man groaned under his ministrations.

"Now perhaps we'll be able to get some answers," I said to Sven and Seraph.

"I vould hope so, Major," said Sven, "for that man is Olaf, my brother."

Half an hour later and after Jones had finished his work and reported in, the news was not especially promising.

"I've done my best and made him as comfortable as I can, sir. Funny looking wound, went clean through his side, like it wasn't made by a bullet at all. He's stable now, but weak, so go gently if you can."

"Understood. Sven, you heard? He's all yours."

"Ja Major. I vill translate as we go along." And so as Olaf's tale began to unfold, we gathered closer and listened intently as Sven solemnly intoned his brother's tale, though the burr of his Norwegian accent I will not attempt to replicate.

CHAPTER FOUR: OLAF'S SAGA

"They came a month ago with no warning, SS in lorries, half-tracks and snow bikes, but no ordinary SS these with their Black Suns and strange weapons. But why? That is what we wondered. What could they want with such a remote and isolated village miles from anywhere – and on the Finnish side of the border? We could not begin to guess and Maalia was afraid that they had come for me. I told her 'don't be foolish woman, they would not send a whole army for one poor Norwegian'. It made no sense.

But they rousted out the whole village that morning, made us all stand and listen while their leader, a small, wicked looking man with a face like a fox and a single eye, attempted to reassure us. "We mean you no harm," he said, in an apparently friendly tone, the one every oppressor uses. "We are simple archaeologists, lovers of history, come to celebrate our shared Aryan heritage with you our Finnish brothers. The Führer has sent us to explore an ancient site to the north of here, where it is said the ancient gods made their home. These are myths and legends of which you are aware no doubt, but the Führer is a curious man and he likes his curiosity to be indulged."

"I say again, we mean you no harm, allow us to carry out our work in peace and we will treat you well, pay you a fair price for any meat and fish you care to sell us and you will be treated with dignity and honour as befits our Aryan brothers."

"However," and at this he leaned over the half-track where he stood and fixed us with that single, horrible eye, "interfere or hinder us in any way and you will find the Fatherland is not so forgiving, even to those of the same master race. Am I understood?" There was some muttering from the Finns who are a fierce and independent people, but it is not so easy to be defiant when you stand amongst your own women and children and armed men surround you. So with very little grumbling, the villagers dispersed and returned to their homes.

And at first, the *Tyskerne*, the Germans, were as good as their word. They had brought slave workers, Poles, Romanies, Ukrainians, and Jews, and they began to build a camp to the north of here at the base of the mountain they call *Odin's Nrykin* or Odin's Fist.

Now, local legends say that in Viking times there was a great temple up there inside the summit, an underground palace in the hollow hill where the hanged god used to ride down from Valhalla and preside over great feasts, combats, and even orgies in his honour. They say that the Allfather would descend to entertain heroes and uncanny creatures of this and even other worlds, hearing their tales and learning their wisdoms in his endless quest for knowledge. Local men from the region served him, becoming priests of Odin known as Drottnar or 'rulers' who would arrange great sacrifices of hanged men and beasts in the gallows god's honour.

They were dark, savage times when the outside world trembled and asked, 'Who will save us from the wrath of the Norsemen?' and here, the cult of Odin grew and flourished. The Drottnar became ever more powerful, controlling the people and even commanding the local Jarls. Then for a long while it is said Odin came to this place no more, abandoning his priests as he fought a great war in the heavens against the frost giants.

In the long years of his absence, the Drottnar grew ever more powerful, forgetting their god, abandoning or perverting his rites, and seeking esoteric knowledge of their own. It is said they summoned the dead and entertained and even interbred with creatures from the outer spheres.

Yet the Allfather is a jealous god and he does not forget, for he is the father of lies and deception as well as wisdom. When he had fought and won his great war, he sent his ravens Huggin and Muninn to spy on the mortal realm and very quickly he learned of the Drottnar's heresy. Once he had recovered from his many wounds, the Allfather mounted his great eight-legged horse Sleipnir and brandishing his mighty war spear Gungnir, descended up the temple and fell upon the faithless Drottnar, who had served him so unfaithfully. His revenge was as terrible and poetic as you would expect from the master of the runes.

As their lord had once endured, so were the Drottnar hanged for nine days to teach them the wisdom of pain. When he cut them down, each was transformed into a terrible, half mad ice demon, an eternal sleepless guardian, cursed it is said, to forever guard the hanged god's greatest treasure in the old hollow hill.

All of this was forgotten in the taming of the Norsemen by Christianity and it was only once recorded in the dark and blasphemous *Uriglegand's Saga*, a tale which was though to have vanished from the face of the earth some nine centuries ago.

But the North does not forget and the tale was also passed from father to son through the ages, to be told around the fires to scare the children and keep them from playing on the mountain. I had heard the stories of Odin's demons of course, for the winter here is long and dark and one must amuse oneself as one can, but like most, I thought it just some unsavoury folk tale. Few enough would venture onto the mountain anyway, not during daylight and certainly not at night, for even without its evil reputation, it is a treacherous enough place naturally, full of piercing gusts, sudden snowstorms, rock falls, and deep crevasses. There is nothing there anyway apart from some ancient caves, so what is to be gained from exploring it? 'Pff, let the Nazis have their stupid game' I thought. If we are lucky, maybe an avalanche will wipe them from the face of the earth and it will save us the trouble of killing them ourselves."

At this point Olaf lapsed into a coughing fit which brought blood seeping through his bandages and his face took on an awful pallor. His brow beaded with sweat and his eyes dimmed growing worryingly opaque.

"Should we let him rest?" I wondered aloud, but Olaf coughed something out in Norwegian and Sven translated. "No, he says, he says he must finish Major, before it is too late."

"Where's that brandy, Bennett?"

"If you'll allow me, Major?" said Seraph and moving to the bed, gently laid his hands across the stricken man's temples. Perhaps it was a trick of the light in there, but for a moment I swear they seemed to glow with a golden light and Olaf tensed, as if he had received some kind of electrical shock. Yet when Seraph was done the transformation was remarkable. Where he seemed about to embrace the arms of death, Olaf's skin had now regained much of its colour and while he was still weak, his eyes were clear and bright and his voice had regained some of its vigour.

"He says, 'thank you' Mister Seraph, but he vould also appreciate some of ze brandy… for medicinal purposes of course." Seraph smiled, I nodded, and Bennett dispensed the tot which Olaf glugged down with relish. Somewhat revived, he resumed his tale with Sven once again translating.

"For a week or two, nothing really gave us much cause for concern. The Nazis confined themselves to their camp at the base of the mountain, occasionally visiting to buy meat and milk and always paying a handsome price. So, despite some muttering, few complained.

It began one Wednesday, Odin's day, on that ill-omened night the Finns name the eve of wandering souls. We had seen the glow of electrical lights and torches earlier in the evening, which told us the Nazis had moved onto the mountain in force, but what their purpose was we could only guess. Then for a few hours all became quiet.

"Just before midnight, it began. At first it was easy to dismiss it as just a localised storm, for, while on the mountain the winds howled and snow began to blanket the peak, down here in the valley, all was calm and still, as if the earth was listening.

"Then the lightning came and as we sat drinking in Juri's, some of the younger men joked that perhaps it was Thor rather than Odin who had returned to haunt the mountain. Old Juri though was ill at ease and cantankerous, cursing the Nazis for messing with forces they couldn't comprehend and berating the younger men as fools and lack wits. But the drinks flowed and this storm passed and the next morning, much was the same as it ever was. In the cold light of day it was easy to shrug off Juri's warning that 'they have stirred what should not be stirred' as an old man's ravings. But the next night and for all the nights that followed, it was not so easy to dismiss the happenings as simple superstition.

"Every night the mountain seemed to breed new and darker events. Weird lights glowed around the peak, sudden snow storms came and went, and the wind carried the sound of wailing as if a multitude were in great pain. So each night the villagers locked and bolted their doors and huddled deeper in their beds and many were afraid to even cast their gaze towards Odin's Fist, lest they attract the evil eye upon their house. And the dogs, my god, the dogs! How they howled and snarled, growled and whimpered, bared their teeth and raised their hackles as if the very legions of hell were knocking on the door. We had to lock them up outside in the end, lest they bite someone in their fear.

"When next the Nazis came to the village, everyone ran inside and locked their doors. No-one would deal with them now, no matter how much they offered and I watched as a Feldwebel and his two Black Sun troopers marched away, cursing us for fools and *untermensch* and promising we would serve the Fatherland soon enough. Something in those words chilled me and I resolved that I must find out more about what was happening up there, both for the sake of the village and because I know you British would be interested in these unusual happenings. This much I conveyed to you in the radio message, but when Maalia saw me readying my hunting gear and weapons, she wept and wailed almost as much as the beasts. I told her 'Woman, this is war. Someone needs to go and it must be me.'

"Yet even though it must be done, I was not ready to make an assault on the mountain single-handedly. The place to begin was obviously the German camp and so as the sun began to fade beneath the horizon, I set out through the trees, to discover just what those Nazis had been meddling with.

"I am not a nervous man or of a superstitious disposition, but with the fading of the light my apprehension grew and I felt an odd tingle, as if some ancient instinct were warning me of the horrors to come. But I dismissed it, 'Olaf,' I said, 'there is a mission to be accomplished and a war to be won, this is not the time to give in to the primitive night terrors,' but I am not sure I sounded convincing, even to myself.

"So when I shivered, it was not entirely against the cold, but I came to their camp without incident and hid myself up a tree, so I could observe their comings and goings. I could see the Nazis or rather their slave workers had been busy, clearing the trees and erecting a fortified compound beneath the shadow of the peak.

"An unbroken perimeter of wire and wood enclosed field tents and vehicles, and at each corner, a watchtower's searchlight cut through the gloom, making the night like day. Twin machine gun nests guarded the entrance and the perimeter was regularly patrolled by masked Black Sun in heavy capes and mountain survival gear. If this was a mere archaeological expedition, then my aunt is Hitler's favourite general. This was more like a fortified prisoner of war camp, prepared for trouble inside as well as out.

"And so I observed for a few hours, but there was nothing very much to report. The guards made their rounds, were relieved, went inside and ate, and nothing much else changed. I was just on the verge of climbing down and returning home, when there was a small commotion and about twenty Black Sun assembled in front of a big tent near the centre of the compound. The leader, the one eyed man, said something to them and then they dived inside there was much shouting of '*Raus! Raus!*'

"Tumbling out came the labourers, though far fewer than those we had seen when they came past the village and the Nazis forced them into a parody of a parade where they stood trembling in their thin striped pyjamas and yellow stars. It was not just the cold, they looked tired and haggard, haunted too, as if they knew some terrible fate awaited them. The one-eyed leader spoke to them, taunting them, I think, I do not understand that accursed language very well, but he said something about them finally having a chance to serve the Fatherland properly.

"On his order, the SS used their rifle butts and began to drive those unfortunates toward the gates. But despite the kicks and blows, they were reluctant to move, until one of the SS took a pistol out and just shot one clean through the head. He lay where he fell.

"Poor bastards. It was a pitiful sight watching them being herded like beasts to the slaughter and for a moment I raised my rifle and sighted it ready to put a bullet straight through that Nazi bastard's eye. Yet it would not have saved a single one of them and would have shown my hand and I had more to think about, Maalia, the rest of the village, and getting word back to you. Still, it was not easy to watch and do nothing as they were pushed and forced and kicked up the path which leads towards the mountain.

"My heart weighed like an anvil on my way back, but this is war and now, I could only think of what I must do next. Whatever the Nazis were up to up there, it was important, that much was certain. They do not march into the wilderness and build an armed base on a mere whim. Sven and ultimately London must be told. And what about the noises, lights, and strange activity up on the mountain? Surely there couldn't be any truth in those folk tales? Yet what else could it be and what lurked up there in the darkness that made the labourers so afraid that it took a bullet to get them to move? Why were there so few of them left? All of these thoughts pounded through my head, but worst of all the Feldwebel's words came back to me, echoing one-eye's, and I hurried my step.

"I was half way back at the village when it began and this time the mountain seemed to explode in a fury of light and sound, as if the underworld itself were being ripped to the surface and the demons of hell unleashed to dance upon it. I was so distracted I hardly noticed the sounds until they were nearly upon me, footsteps rushing through the snow and I just had time to duck behind a tree as they drew closer. I drew my knife and as he ran past, I stuck out a foot, brought him down and buried both knees into his back, my hand ramming his head into the earth, ready to plunge the point through his shoulder blades.

"But this was no Nazi I had brought down. The striped pyjamas, forage cap, and pitifully starved frame quickly told me that. It was one of the labourers, an escapee who now struggled and squirmed and whimpered beneath me. I rolled off as gently as I could, trying to make reassuring sounds in the few words of German that I have, but as soon as I was off him, he swung at my throat with a piece of glass that had been concealed in his hand. I barely managed to deflect it with my rifle and on instinct cracked him with the butt, felling him.

'Nicht Deutche! Nicht Deutche! Widerstand… resistance ja?'

"Eyes flashing like a feral cat, he tried to rise again, but the muzzle of my rifle persuaded him to stay put and now I could see that this was no he at all, but a woman, for the Nazis are no respecters of sex. We stared at each other for a long moment and then she seemed to realise I meant her no harm and began to babble away in German. She kept repeating the word '*Schrecken*' which I think means 'horror.' It was not easy to understand her, for she was plainly terrified, but then she threw away the shard of glass and began to sob, and then crawled closer and hugged my leg.

"She was a sorry sight, pitifully thin and shivering with the cold. I quickly stripped off my sweater and gave it to her, then searched my pockets and found some chocolate which I handed over. She stared at me as if she had forgotten the meaning of human kindness and then began to eat like a starved wolf. For a moment I was at a loss, what should I do now? It is one thing to watch people led away to their fate at a distance, but when you are confronted by a real person, right there in front of you? I could not abandon her, what choice did I have?

"But would the Nazis come looking? Would they notice one escaped prisoner with all the commotion up on the mountain? I could not tell, but one thing was for certain if they did, they would go straight to the village, for there was nowhere else in this wilderness and they must not find us there. So, after she had finished the chocolate, I helped her to her feet and then motioned her to come with me. For a moment she didn't seem to understand, and then I held out my hand and she took it and we began our march through the woods.

"Our progress was slow, for most of the strength seemed to have been taken from her and she was a little delirious I think, for she kept up a low keening, like a child anxious for its mother. And she kept looking back, always looking back to the mountain. Even though that peak itself had fallen silent, there was a strange quality to the woods now, a tension, as if Mother Nature herself were holding her breath. I am a hunter and have spent most of my life under the trees and I felt something was not right, as if all life, from the beasts to the birds, had suddenly fled before some strange premonition of evil.

"We hurried on and I was almost dragging her along now and then I felt it, an odd sensation as if someone, or perhaps something had latched onto our trail and was actively seeking us out. Call it instinct, but I've learned to trust these feelings and she seemed to feel it too and hauled at my arm and said that phrase again and her eyes were wide with terror. In an instant my plan changed, there was no going to the village now, we must cross the river, douse our scent in the cold of the water, erase our tracks, and make for a local cave where I knew we could hole up. On and on we ran, pulses pounding as one and we forgot all weariness, all tiredness in our eagerness to get away, for I knew we must shake this horrible, unknown pursuer at any cost. To hesitate or pause for even an instant would mean death or something even worse.

"The trees tore and rent our clothes, the brush snagged and snarled and we abandoned all pretence of stealth in our headlong flight. Inexplicably, I could feel it coming closer, cold, relentless, unfeeling, like the very breath of winter made flesh. At full tilt I half turned my head, but I could see nothing and yet I felt it still, like the doe feels the hot breath of the mountain lion on her neck.

Then our feet were splashing in the icy water. The river! We stumbled in the shallows and using every last shred of my remaining energy, I hauled her through the water and we waded downstream sapped by the bitter chill. We flowed with the river, letting its gentle chatter disguise our steps and even though I cast anxious glances behind and listened for any sign of pursuit, now, I could detect nothing.

"A few hundred metres down, near the top of a small waterfall, we halted for a moment and I gave her a thumbs up, which brought a ragged smile to that terrified face. I put my finger to my lips then pointed across the river and she nodded and we waded across, taking care to keep low and silent and avoid the slippery rocks.

"We emerged dripping onto the far shore and I listened again, casting my eyes upstream. Nothing. Perhaps we had eluded it? We were just a couple of metres away from the shelter of the trees and then the safety of the cave. I held out my hand, smiled again, but now she shrank away from me, as if I were some kind of horror and then I realised it was not I, but something behind me that inspired her terror. Her mouth opened in a soundless scream and I was turning, finger pumping, firing blindly into the dark…

"A great fire erupted in my side and I thought I was shot through, but when I looked down, two great spikes of ice had pierced my side. I grunted with the pain, falling to my knees and dropping the rifle. I tried to shout, but it was as if all the breath had been stolen from me. She stood there in the water, immobile, frozen in her terror and I can remember there was an overwhelming musky smell, and then a giant white furred hand with wicked talons reached out and seized her, enveloping her head completely and lifted her clean off the ground. In my pain, I struggled to turn and see what it was, but she… they were gone and I was left alone there, bleeding my life out into the snow. I had not even known her name…"

At this point Olaf was seized by a coughing fit and it took several moments for Bennett to calm him again, he did not look well, most of the colour had drained from his face and he was as pale as the snow. Bennett hastily applied more brandy which allowed him to rally him and then he resumed.

"For a while, I hovered between life and death, but the pain won out and using my rifle as a crutch, I managed to half-stagger, half-crawl into the cave behind the waterfall, where I had laid stores and provisions as a precaution if I ever needed to flee the Germans. I lit the fire against the cold and found the spikes had melted away and I was able to staunch the blood flow and cauterise and bind the wound before my strength left me. I slept for a long time, perhaps a day, perhaps two, I do not know, but when I awoke again, I was weak. I struggled to come back to the village, but found it deserted, all the people had gone. You have seen the dogs? Whatever abomination did that to them, is the same as did this to me. You must stop them, Sven, find them, bring Maalia back to me. I…"

Now, Olaf was very weak and he sank back into the pillow, regarding us through fever-bright eyes. He was spent and Bennett signalled that we should sedate him. I nodded, for it seemed there was little more he could tell us.

"Rest easy, brother, rest," said Sven. "We will find her for you and the rest of them, or we will die in the attempt. I promise it. It shall be so." Olaf nodded at brother's vow and then fell unconscious.

"A dark tale, Seraph. What do you make of it?" I asked and Seraph took a moment before he spoke, carefully weighing what he had heard.

"It is as I feared, it seems von Obertorff has been meddling with forces he shouldn't, summoning beings that should no longer walk upon the face of this Earth. But to what end? That is the question we should be asking, what is his ultimate purpose? And that I don't yet know. Clearly the mountain has significance, but we need more information. Perhaps we might find it at the Nazi camp? That should be our next port of call. Can we reconnoitre it in daylight without being detected?"

"That we can. Sergeant Jones go and fetch Barker, we'll move out in five minutes."

"And Olaf?"

"He vill be content enough here, Mister Seraph. Vun way or the other, we can do nothing more for him for now."

It is perhaps a measure of how far we had come that I had accepted Olaf's tale and Seraph's analysis of it without demur. We seemed to have been transported to a place where the strange and uncanny became the commonplace and I think even the men had begun to accept it. We were dealing with forces beyond the normal order of things and Seraph's very otherworldliness became an asset rather than a hindrance. I for one was becoming rather glad we had him on board. Our preparations did not go according to plan though, for Sergeant Jones returned almost instantly and said, "Beg pardon sir, but I think you'd better come see this."

And go see it we did. It proved to be a sight that chilled the marrow. Jones led us back to where Barker had been stationed, but where there should have been a strapping Scotsman, there was nothing except the indentation where his body had lain on the ground. There were no tracks nor signs of a struggle which made no sense, why would he wander off alone? The Section made strong, independent-minded soldiers, but obedient ones too and he would not have abandoned his post without an extremely good reason. A short moment later, Jones provided it. "Found it over there sir, some twenty yards into the trees." He laid the Bren – or the remains of it – down on the ground. The solid metal body of the LMG lay twisted and mangled as if it had been pounded by a steam press.

"Gods! Vot could have done this?"

"The same thing that took the villagers and almost did for poor Olaf, undoubtedly."

"And what would that be, Seraph?"

"At a guess? The 'horror' which the forced worker mentioned, Major, the thing that attacked Olaf."

"And what the hell is that?"

"I'm not sure and I hesitate to speculate without more conclusive data, but nothing human did this, that's for certain. If what I suspect is true, von Obertorff may have disturbed an ancient, sleepless evil, but why? To what end? We need to know more, Major. The sooner we can get to that camp, the better."

"Very well then," I said, "let's waste no more time."

CHAPTER FIVE: CAMP OF THE DAMNED

Late afternoon sunshine speared through the trees as we hiked north in the direction of the Nazi camp. The sun's rays were welcome, for occasionally, through the foliage, we would now catch a glimpse of the mountain which loomed powerful and brooding. Odin's Fist seemed to deserve its evil reputation, for it looked like a cruel and savage peak, full of harsh, angular rock faces crowned with ice. It exuded an aura of deep menace, as if it were a living thing directing its baleful gaze toward us.

There were other matters closer to hand that demanded my attention though, and the need to concentrate on a tangible military objective helped to focus my distracted mind. I had lost a third of my men since this operation began for no good cause and I was determined that we would lose no more, so Sven and I scouted quietly ahead while Bennett and Jones hung back to protect our so-called civilian specialist.

The Nazi camp was fortunately not too difficult to find, for they had hacked a rudimentary road through the forest and once we came across it, we simply followed along its edges, being careful to remain hidden. As we drew closer and caught a first glimpse of its gates, I signalled Sven and the others to circle around the perimeter so we could take a closer look from a more advantageous position. Minutes later, we were hunkered down, observing the place from cover. The camp was much as Olaf had described it, a rectangular enclosure of wooden posts and barbed wire, guarded by a watchtower at each corner with the heavy gates typical of a German forced labour camp.

But even as we crouched there, it was not difficult to detect something was amiss. Though we could hear the low drone of the camp's generators, the gates had been left wide open, swinging on their hinges in the wind and even though the first notes of dusk were just beginning to bleed into the daylight, the full beams of the searchlights arced out, hanging limp from tenantless watch towers. Where we had been expecting to find a fully armed, hostile German base, instead there was no sound, no movement, and no sign of life within. We stayed watching for a while, but when the silence had stretched over many minutes I whispered to Seraph, who seemed to have retreated into one of his trances. "It seems deserted."

"Yes, I don't feel any signs of life."

"Well, we won't get a better chance to take a look around."

"Agreed, but cautiously, Major. We don't know if or when they may return and there may be things here that are beyond even my senses."

"Understood. Corporal Bennett, Sergeant Jones, stay together and see what you can find. Sven, you're with me. What are we looking for, Seraph?"

"We may not know until we find it, but the command post or von Obertoff's quarters would probably be a good place to start."

We circled back to the main gates and with a final look-see to determine if we were truly alone, I ordered the men forward. We moved up at the double, keeping a wary eye on the watch towers until we came to the gates themselves, which hung on their hinges as if they had been thrown open by some great force. Above the lintel someone had written the slogan "Jedem das Seine" but the sign was hanging half off at a crazy angle.

"It means, 'to each his own' or 'to each what he deserves'," said Seraph anticipating my question. "Their idea of a joke, no doubt, but it seems their own cruel taunt may have come back to bite them."

The ground beyond the gate was cut up and marked by ruts and the passage of many feet and vehicles, but when we came to the two machine gun nests, we could see a great many cartridges scattered on the ground and although the MG42s were still in place, they were cold to the touch. There were bloody smears in the snow leading up to and all around the sandbags and everywhere were small scraps of striped material mingled with the blood. Most disturbingly, we could see distinct tracks which resembled long, outsized human feet, with the indentations of large talons beyond the toes. Seraph bent down to examine them and then picked up a lone *Stahlhelm* which had been discarded. The insignia was a circle with angular, radial spikes reminiscent of the swastika, a black sun, but it had been battered and dented as if struck by a fearsome blow.

"Something unusual happened here, something the Nazis weren't expecting. The gates were smashed, thrown open, no easy task you'll agree under heavy machine gun fire. There was a charge, then a desperate hand-to-hand struggle. No survivors and significantly, no bodies."

"This was a fortified position, covered by MG42s. A frontal assault would have been suicide."

"Should have been and yet, not only did they make it through, but they overran these positions and then the rest of the camp."

"Vot!? Are they unaffected by bullets then?"

"Resistant perhaps, and significantly they have also taken the dead, or the living, with them."

"Vot should we do?"

"Keep searching, there are answers here somewhere."

As an uneasy dusk stole over the camp, we searched in the early evening gloom. The peak of Odin's Fist slowly turned the colour of blood as the sun retreated and the mount became a great, dark silhouette, its pernicious influence seeming to cast an ever deeper shadow. Wherever we looked the evidence spoke of the same uneasy story Seraph had described. Blood pooled in the watchtowers, there were more of those sinister footprints and we found twisted guns and rifles which seemed to have been snapped or perhaps even bitten in half. But no bodies, no bodies at all. Something, something desperately savage and powerful, had attacked this camp, overwhelmed the Nazis and then spirited any evidence away. Perhaps we should have been grateful, for it would have been devilish tricky to infiltrate a fully manned and operational base, yet I would not believe that in this case, the enemy of our enemy was our friend.

We found the dismal, primitive conditions where the labourers had been kept, no doubt shivering under thin blankets in light canvas tents, which contrasted sharply with the well-equipped, luxurious quarters of the Black Sun. In the command post, an advanced looking radio hissed static until Bennett shut it off and the maps spread over the table contained a strange mix of archaeological data and esoteric symbols which seemed to dance before the eyes and have an unsettling effect on the mind. I did not mind it at all when Seraph swiftly covered them up with a cloth.

Another half hour's worth of investigation had yielded little more in the encroaching darkness, so we repaired to the command tent again and I set a watch and ordered a break. We'd been on the go since morning and discovered nothing but deeper and darker mysteries. As Sven and the men tucked into their rations, I went outside and brooded over a pipe. Where would it all end? For there seemed little hope of rescuing the villagers or the labourers now, and with the Nazis massacred or removed for some unknown purpose what had our mission become anyway?

I regarded the dark shape of the mountain which loomed over us and could not quite suppress a shiver, feeling that somehow all must all end up there. A hopeless cause and overwhelming odds I could face with the blithest of spirits, that's par for the course in the Section, but how do you fight a supernatural enemy who could apparently breeze through a camp of heavily armed SS veterans with scarcely a pause for breath?

"You fight them the same way you fight all of our enemies, with courage, tenacity, and the good old British stiff upper lip, if you must. How are you bearing up, Major?" Seraph seemed to materialise at my elbow from nowhere.

"That is a most unnerving habit, Seraph."

"My apologies, Major, but I believe I may have found something that might just help. Something that may just explain the mystery at the heart of this affair and perhaps even help tilt the balance in our favour."

"And what would that be?"

"Von Obertorff's journal. Come, let's go see exactly what that Nazi madman has been up to."

Moments later, we were back inside and Seraph spread the book out on the map table. It was an old dark leather tome, covered in strange arcane symbols. Seraph made a couple of passes with his hands over it, muttering under his breath and then 'It' opened of its own accord seeming to give an audible sigh as the yellowing pages were revealed. Natural curiosity urged me to take a peek, but Seraph placed a protective arm across my chest. "It's written in a mix of German, old Norse, and some rather malevolent looking runes, probably safest if I translate." And so as the shadows lengthened, he did.

"February 12th — We have arrived in the middle of this Finnish wilderness, beneath the shadow of Odin's Fist. It is the site, I am certain of it, for having consulted the map and now having seen it, no other bears the characteristic shape named in Uriglegand's Saga. *How fortunate we are that that forgotten, forbidden text has so recently come to light in the library that was thought lost.*

Or perhaps it is more than fortunate, perhaps it is destiny after all that has led us here? For I must confess I feel the spirit of our pagan ancestors at work and the hand of our Aryan forefathers on my shoulder. After our recent reverse in Russland it must be a sign, a gift left for us, hidden down the long centuries for our time of need. If my interpretation is correct, the Führer will be most pleased, for if we attain our goal, even if the Americans enter the war here in mainland Europe, we would be irresistible. I can scarcely contain myself from exploring the mountain right way.

But to practicalities first. We have found a suitable site at the base of the mountain and the untermensch have been put to work building a camp. I have also addressed the local peasants in the village. It is difficult to believe these people are part of the same master race, but even the purest line may have degenerate branches I suppose. They seemed cowed by our display of arms and fierce Aryan will. I do not expect any trouble from these peasants, but if there is, I will suppress it with a ferocity that they will never forget. Nothing must be allowed to compromise my mission. Nothing.

February 15th – The mountain is harsh and unforgiving, but I have discovered the ancient sacrificial road which the Norsemen must have used and it provides a steep, but ready means to attain the peak. The summit Itself is hollow and contains an extensive cave system like a honeycomb and although there is much evidence of pagan occupation, I have found a central temple-like complex devoted to Odin. I have yet to discover the inner sanctuary the saga mentions. Perhaps further meditation upon the text will help me uncover its secrets?

Down below, much progress has been made on the camp and we are secure now, safe within our wire walls and fences. I constantly have to remind the men not to work the labourers too hard or treat them too badly, much as it goes against their instincts. I wonder if they think me too merciful? Nothing could be further from the truth. The rituals may require much blood and many lives, and we need to retain a fresh supply of both at hand.

February 16th - I have unearthed the inner sanctum and now I believe our glorious Aryan ancestors meant me to find this place. What irony that one of the untermensch discovered it, although he paid with his life when the tunnel collapsed around him. The first of many sacrifices I suspect.

The rock fall exposed an old half-collapsed tunnel and I ordered the men to wait on the threshold while I explored alone. A long passage winds down for many metres into the very innards of the mountain to reveal the great secret of this place. For there in a vast hollow cavern, lit by a pale, unnatural luminescence which seems to seep from the rock itself, lies a hidden temple sacred to the hanged god carved into the mountain's heart stone. A malevolent grove of twisted trees surrounds the huge heart Ash at its centre and the roof above seems to stretch away into the stars, as if you were peering out into the void of the heavens.

I stared in wonder for a long timeless space, mesmerised by the weird unnatural beauty of this place which I imagine no mortal must had laid eyes on for long centuries. As if waking or perhaps entering a trance, I approached the great tree itself whose roots seemed to dig deep into the mountain. I gazed at its empty, leafless branches and the gnarled trunk which seemed to have sprung from the seed of the world tree itself for a long while, before I saw them, the unnatural shapes below.

They were spread around the base like numbers on a clock face, each entombed within its own prison of ice. Then suddenly I could hear or perhaps feel it, a mind reaching out to me, a deep, exotic consciousness that whispered of scenes from the past centuries. There were no words, just visions of when the Norsemen had worshipped the old ways here, blood rituals and terrible sacrifices to honour the hanged god and his disciples from beyond this world. Then it spoke of release, of freedom, and showed me the way, revealing the dark rites necessary to unlock those chains of ice which contained it and its fellows — and it promised great rewards, untold treasures, the shining spear for the one who would release them, the one who would release the Drottnar.

February 18th — The time nears to begin the awakening, yet the process both troubles and fascinates me. The ritual is complicated, yes, but I believe it is within my scope and while It calls for many lives, that is not my concern. The untermensch will serve in this as they have served in everything else...

No, It is the creature itself which gives me pause, for whilst it roamed in my mind I was also simultaneously able to see a little into its own. This is no mythical creature sprung from Norse legends, but a being from another world which once roamed this Earth and interbred with our Aryan ancestors. It is these hybrids, the Drottnar, these strange beings which now form the court which is frozen alongside it.

I am surprised at how little this cosmological revelation troubles me; that creatures from another world exist and walked amongst us should not be a shock to the rational mind. It is merely confirmation of what I have always suspected. We are not alone and now I have the proof of it. That they should have shaped our Aryan ancestors should also be no revelation, they simply grafted themselves onto the true stem of our own master race.

February 20th — Even after two day's reflection, intense study of the Saga's text and the protective wards, I know I must proceed carefully. Even in its icy shroud, one can discern the immense physical power of the creature. What would Rascher make of this? He will be most envious. Yet it is the subtle, savage intelligence of its mind which makes one shudder. This is a being not easily controlled or manipulated and it will always ultimately pursue its own purposes. I could feel it attempt to impose its will on my own and while I allowed it to believe it had dominated me, my actions and thoughts were perhaps not entirely of my own choosing.

Chapter Five: Camp of the Damned   49

Yet the prize it offers is immense and tantalising and no truly great endeavour is ever free of risk. I must prepare well and venture much, including my own safety if necessary, if I am to succeed. Yet I believe the counter-spells and enchantments will hold. They must. If I can secure the artefact and even a fraction of this being's knowledge, the Reich's ultimate victory will be assured. The Führer's gratitude will know no bounds.

February 21st – Success! Success beyond even my wildest imaginings. My hand is shaking so much I can barely commit the words to paper, but I have made history. I, Ludwig von Obertorff, will be remembered as one of the foremost heroes of the Reich for this night's work, worthy to be spoken of in the same breath as the Führer himself in the thousand year reign.

I have not only freed the Drottnar, but bound it too, with dark unspeakable sorceries, so it cannot leave the confines of the temple against my will. Now, if I can overmaster it, all its knowledge and power will be pressed into the Fatherland's service and it will ensure our ultimate triumph against those lesser races who would drag us back into their own squalor...

I still tremble, for it was no easy feat and nearly blasted my very soul. Outside, the very air itself seemed to spasm, the storm lashing the peak and unmanning men and the workers alike, as I conjured the infernal powers. Even with the additional eldritch energy of this foul night, it drained my will to a point where it was only with the greatest difficulty I could return. I feel as if part of my soul has been given up unto it and I have received something powerful yet terrible in return…

We had to expend over half the untermensch to free the Drottnar from its bonds, but they had served their purpose and are now no longer a drain on our supplies. Even though they were inferiors, it was no easy thing to watch them dangle one by one in that cursed grove. Yet, it was a necessary sacrifice and the Drottnar is risen. Now I must rest, for tomorrow begins a new and terrible era in the history of mankind..

February 23rd – The creature is as malevolent as Loki and as cunning as Odin himself, but we have shared our thoughts and It has allowed me to peer into its mind and experience its consciousness. Yet always I can feel it contend with me, seeking an advantage, a chance to overpower me, to break the enchantments.

I watched as its kind first visited this realm when the Norsemen turned the Northlands red with their reaving. Finding the local gods to their liking, they adopted and perverted the local cult of Odin, mingling their blood with its priests and borrowing the old Norse name of Drottnar or 'rulers'. For decades, perhaps centuries, this hollow hill was their home and with their human allies and unholy children, they ruled, demanding fealty and sacrifice from bondsmen, freeman, and Jarl alike.

Then they could slip more easily between the worlds, but why were this one and its hybrids left behind? I must know more. But It demands more lives, more sacrifices to free them and it whispers of the sacred artefact, a most tempting prize. I must be cautious and not allow it to deceive me, for if what I have seen is true, then it would prove a most potent weapon, allowing us to strike at London, New York, or even Washington. Its potential is far beyond anything we might have dreamt of with the work at Peenemunde.

February 25th – Our minds grow closer, intermingled. It has shown me many secrets, mysteries of the higher universe that are almost unimaginable, inconceivable to the mortal mind and too terrible to share. I have seen... ach, but words fail me, lesser beings are not ready for this knowledge.

I feel my body begin to transform, change and in my dreams, I hear its whispers now, its promises of how we might rule together. I should resist, but it grows ever more compelling... In a vision It has shown me the sacred lance, which the Norsemen called Gungnir, the swaying one, that they thought was the spear of Odin. But it is a weapon that dwarfs our feeble conceptions of armaments. To control it would be to hold sway over the world and shake the capitals of Axis and Allies alike.

I, we, must have it. Yet the Drottnar has also revealed to me the one who is coming, the one who has watched us from afar, this one who would thwart us. He wishes to spy on us with his hateful magics but we have prevented it and we must make all preparations against this pallid witchman.

February 26th – I... the Drottnar weakens and needs to feed and I expended the last of the untermensch to supplement ou—its life force. Once again, they were taken to the grove and bound to the trees, but the weaker amongst the SS had little stomach for it and I was forced to turn hangman myself. Curious how they kick and struggle even as the noose tightens, hanging onto life until the very last breath…

Yet for all our precautions, one had somehow escaped and weak from the magics, or open to its suggestions, I freed the Drottnar from the confines of the mountain and allowed it to pursue her out into the wider world. For a while I was fearful that having unleashed it, it would never return, but then I seemed to see through its eyes, relentlessly stalking, hunting, seizing its prey. She was petrified with terror, whispering 'horror' over and over again. She scarcely seemed to notice as I tightened the noose. When the fall broke her neck… I think it was a great relief to her.

February 27th – Perhaps it has grown less cautious or perhaps I have begun to understand it more, for I have seen into an unguarded corner of its mind, seen how the Norsemen overthrew its kind and imprisoned it here in the ice.

For long ages the Drottnar dominated and overshadowed the land, but when its disciples grew greedy, when they called for the Norsemen's own sons and daughters, rather than their mere bondsmen and slaves, for their sacrifices, then the Vikings could endure no more.

Steeled by the runic magics of a great gathering of witchmen and skalds, the Norsemen stormed the unholy mountain and put the Drottnar and its progeny to the sword in a great night of blood and fire. Most of its fellows fled through the world tree, the ladder to the stars, but this one and its offspring were not so fortunate and were trapped here, entombed by the witchmen's magics as a warning to the rest not to return. Without Uriglegand's accursed saga, it would remain here still, but its faithful acolyte would not abandon it and left instructions on how to revive it in his tale. For what has survived down the long ages, we have great cause to thank that ill-starred rogue.

February 28th – It's hunger is a tangible thing now and after long centuries unfed, it needs more souls, more sacrifices to sustain its life force on this plane. Without an active world tree, its connection to the higher dimensions is severed and it must feed more frequently, especially now that we have also awoken some of the hybrids.

March 1st – Even when we are not joined, I hear its voice in my thoughts and I wonder if my mind is truly still my own? My flesh begins to melt and bend under its influence, yet I have never felt such clarity, it is as if I have awoken from my sleep, arisen, like the Drottnar, to see the world with new eyes.

I see more of the witchman now too, he wears the khaki of our enemies and his hair is long, but his face is hidden. He travels under the sea and over the frozen wave and he would prevent m—the Reich's triumph. He brings his hounds of war and white magics to thwart us, but they shall not prevail and he will perish in untold agonies, I swear it.

March 2nd – We have begun the great magic to unlock the spear, but it will be no easy task as the skalds protected it with potent spells and sorcery.

Yet we must feed again, our appetites become insatiable and we have no more untermensch, so I have come to a decision, for the good of the Reich and the continuation of our cause, I will allow them to take the Finnish villagers. I know they are our distant cousins and we share the same racially pure bloodline, but we are too close now to let sentiment overtake us. Let us pay with this last tranche of lives then, if that is what it takes, a small cell sacrificed, so the greater body may endure.

March 3rd – The Drottnar and its acolytes are renewed and its power waxes greatly with the glut of new souls. In this as in everything our great Aryan purity proves superior to the lesser races. It has reanimated some of the hanged villagers to serve it in our great endeavour. Their broken necks click when they walk and shamble, a most curious sound.

As I write these words I wonder if my sanity is still intact for I have seen such things… done such … Have I awoken a creature which will ensure the triumph of the Reich or overwhelm it and perhaps the world itself? And if such things can truly be said to exist, what of my own soul? How will von Obertorff be weighed by the scales of history?

Weak, foolish, pathetic thoughts, unworthy of an Übermensch. *As my body becomes something new, why should I question the triumph of my will? Together, I, me, we, will construct a Reich that will rule for ten millennia and that weak and foolish little Austrian Gefreiter and his Berlin sycophants will perish in the flames. The final solution? It is only a beginning.…*

Yet this nemesis, this witchman also draws closer. I can feel his unholy presence in every step he makes upon the snow. Perhaps our conventional forces can be marshalled against him? I will send word.

March 4th – We are so close now, so close, the shackles are so very nearly thrown off, yet the Drottnar weakens and its-our-my thirst grows ever more insistent. Our minds have grown even closer together and I begin to take on its very shape and form. I believe the Black Sun see it and they begin to fear me as much as the creature. What have I become?

March 5th – At last, we almost shattered the enchantment, but our supreme effort savagely weakened the Drottnar, killed nearly all of the hybrids and most of the reanimated villagers. We must have more power to fuel our magics and there is… but one place to find it.

They are loyal Aryan soldiers, yet this is war and I must have no qualms about what must be done. When the sun sets I will unleash the Drottnar and the remaining hybrids upon the camp before their energy is utterly expended. The Black Sun will pay the toll, but they will be transformed, reborn to serve us. It is the only way…

He too is near now, the pale one, the witchman, so close I can almost smell him, but it will be too late, too late. Tonight, my… our great work will be complete, Gungnir will be released and the worlds will tremble at our coming.

"This last entry was dated yesterday," said Seraph, putting the journal down with a heavy thud. The abrupt break in the narrative startled me, I hadn't realised it, but my body was tense like a coiled wire and the shadows in the tent seemed to form a sinister chorus.

"A most macabre and incredible tale, can we really believe all this? Has this von Obertorff not just gone completely insane?"

"Possibly, but what is sanity, Major?"

"Vikings, aliens, a super weapon concealed in the mists of history and brought back to conquer the world? This mission may have forced me to reconsider many things, Seraph, but it sounds to me like he's gone, well, doolally."

"Ever the sceptic, eh, Major? Yet something attacked Olaf, took the villagers, wiped out the Black Sun."

"Something that knows ve are coming also, if this journal is to be believed," reflected Sven in his dour way. "Yet somehow ve remain alive and this von Obertorff, these Drottnar allies and this weapon, this spear of Odin, has not emerged to strike us down."

"Yes, I'm glad you picked up on that, Sven," said Seraph. "Something's not quite right is it? He's unleashed an ancient evil, raised an ice demon and unlocked a weapon of ultimate power? So where is he? I mean we're all still stood here aren't we, and that at least bodes well."

"So Seraph, what now? Another stroll into the lion's den?"

"This time it's you who's read my mind. Precisely Major, but before we do, come this way, there's something I discovered while I was having a root around in their armoury that I want to show you."

And so, a short while later, as dusk spread its cloak around the mountain, we gathered ourselves for a final assault on von Obertorff's lair. Now I am no choker and not easily spooked, yet even I felt strange misgivings as we set out on the path up towards that ominous peak. I had seen much to shake my complacent scepticism about the supernatural in the past few days and now we seemed ready to beard evil in its very lair, in an away fixture that could determine the course of the war, if not the fate of the world. Yet as I shouldered my Sten and shifted the weight of my pack behind me, the solid frames of Sven, Corporal Bennett, and Sergeant Jones were reassuring. They were stalwart salt-of-the-earth lads and this combined with Seraph's mystical genius meant we at least had a fighting chance. Whatever awaited us up there, if it could be killed, we'd kill it, and if we failed, well, it didn't sound as if there'd be much of a world left to be worth saving.

The path started out smoothly enough, a gentle curve which wended its way ever upward and we were soon swallowed up beneath the gaunt shadows of the pines. Ever alert, we marched stolidly on for some twenty minutes, but there seemed little point in concealment now. As the light ebbed away, the path narrowed and steepened and the going became harder, with loose stones and shale making our footing uncertain. The path zigged and zagged, and then a biting wind seemed to spring up from nowhere, ushering in a chilling, sapping mist that engulfed us in moments. Suddenly path, landmarks, and mountain alike were lost, as if we had been deposited into a glass of gaseous milk.

"Someone seems to be expecting us. We should rope ourselves together for safety," said Seraph and I nodded the order. Bound together like a chain gang groping its way across a darkened cellar, we progressed a footstep at a time, battling against the stellar cold and the lack of visibility alike. Seraph took the lead and although his eyes seemed to be focussed on things beyond the normal sphere of perception, he led us true, step by hard won step, up that perilous path. For a long, timeless interval the world became a white-out haze, as we struggled to place one foot in front of the other, slogging against the slope, the debilitating wind, and the strange death-like chill of the mist. After what seemed like a small eternity of frozen heartbeats, but may have been five minutes or five hundred, Seraph turned the strange witch light fading from his eyes.

"We're here. This is the entrance to the temple." Beyond him I could just about make out the outline of an entrance, a rocky maw which led into the heart of the mountain.

"Ack thank the gods, I would rather face a legion of unholy monsters, than another second of this accursed mist," said Sven.

"I too," said Seraph, "yet I believe we have not come through unscathed and it has already claimed a victim. I'm sorry Major." As Jones came staggering in beside us, weighed beneath the burden of his heavy pack, I saw the rope behind him was empty, played out, neatly severed where Bennett should have been. At this, I must confess I lost it a little and began to rant, swearing and cursing, and calling down the most terrible vengeance on von Obertorff, the Drottnar and possibly even the ancient Vikings as well. Little good it would have done me or any of us, but Seraph left me to vent for a moment, before grasping me firmly by the shoulders.

"Save your strength, save your hatred, Major. We will need every ounce of it." Something in those eyes and the reassuring tone of his voice exuded a calming influence which brought me back from the brink. I nodded my acquiescence.

CHAPTER SIX: THE TRELLBORG MONSTROSITIES

We stumbled into the entrance of the cave and almost immediately the effects of the mist seemed to dissipate, freeing our bodies and minds from its unholy influence. We unroped ourselves and our flashlights flickered along the uneven surface of the ceiling, sending shadows racing across the rock. It was an eerie, ill-starred place, like a great throat leading down into the oesophagus of the mountain, but Seraph was soon off at a pace, as if he were a hound finally unleashed and hot on the scent of his prey. There were many twists and side tunnels, but he didn't deviate or hesitate for a moment and seemed to pick his way down unerringly. Down and ever down we went and as we progressed, it grew warmer, an unpleasant, moist heat which brought prickles of perspiration to the skin. Soon and much to Seraph's impatience, we were shedding our greatcoats and re-shouldering our heavy packs to stop from boiling up.

Seraph's instinctive pathfinding eventually led us down a wider tunnel and beyond the flickering ovals of our flashlights, I could detect a gradual lightening of the way. The rocks began to glow with a greenish fungal luminescence, faint at first, but growing gradually stronger with every passing stride. The tunnel opened into a great hollow cavern and here, the light from the fungus was strong enough that our torches became superfluous. The signs of Viking occupation were everywhere, with a group of great stone menhirs set in a circle surrounding a vast central stone. Supporting altars had been carved and woven into the rock, with intricate runic symbols and age-worn reliefs recounting the myths and legends of the ancient Norse. This had most likely been the original pagan temple before it had been corrupted and perverted by the Drottnar's monstrous alien creed.

Yet Seraph seemed to have lost both the trail and his certainty and he strode towards the central altar as if sniffing the air to try to pick up the scent again. Watchfully, we surrounded him while he squatted down and disappeared under his cloak to cast the runes, or whatever it is he did under there.

"I am not liking this, I am not liking this at all," said Sven. "I feel as if a thousand eyeballs are crawling across my skin."

"Indeed, if even a quarter of his journal is true, this von Obertorff must surely know we are coming. Why hasn't he done something more substantial to stop us? Why let us get this far? Why pick us off one by one?"

"A very good question, Major. I think you may be about to get an answer." Sven cupped a hand to his ear and then I heard it too, a faint whispering, like the sound of dry twigs being rubbed together. It grew louder and closer, the noises chasing each other around the angular roof of the cave system, echoing and re-echoing, so that they seemed to be coming from everywhere at once. Now the sounds took on a lurching, shuffling nature, like meat and bone collapsing on top of each other and despite my most fervent urgings, Seraph appeared completely oblivious to it all beneath his coverings.

"Very well, looks like it's point defence on, Seraph. Let's get to it, gentlemen," I said with a confidence I didn't feel, while Sven and Jones stood ready and we formed three points of a triangle around our principal.

Out in the shadows beyond the altar, in the dark spaces at the entrances to the cavern, the sounds seemed to cease for a moment, as if whatever was out there was gathering itself. Now, surely, we must see them, whatever they were, we must. Then with a great lurching sigh like an exhalation they burst upon us, lumbering and shuffling forward in a disjointed, staccato parody of a charge, the remains of von Obertorff's Black Sun.

"Fire at will, fire at will!" I shouted, but bursts of gunfire were already drowning out my order. Bullets struck home, raking them, biting into their flesh, sending bodies spinning and jerking with each heavy calibre impact. My Sten kicked as I poured a steady, withering fire into the advancing targets and when the first magazine was spent, I was already ejecting it and ramming home another. Yet where was their return fire? And why did they move so slowly? Most importantly, how the hell were the bodies I'd just downed, starting to rise from the floor of the cavern and lurch forward again?

"Ack zey are dead already, remember. They vill not die! They vill not die again!" exclaimed Sven.

"Aim for the head, sir! Aim for the head!" shouted Jones.

As the creatures lurched to renew their assault, they drew into the arc of the fungal light and now I could see now the soulless, bulging eyes, the swollen necks, and the necrotic hue to their flesh. Some even retained the hempen noose that had ended their life around the neck, and their uneven gait and rickety movements were now explained by the stiffness of death. By god, they stank too, the awful whiff of the charnel house. How we managed to stay even remotely sane at this point I cannot begin to explain.

Yet on they came, no easier to eliminate for all Jones' excellent advice, for it is no simple thing to stay calm and pick your shots with such horrors advancing upon you. And for every one that we downed, two more sprang to take its place and quickly they were upon us at close quarters and there was no time to even reload.

I heard Jones firing, then grunting, then screaming, Sven cursing loudly, but there was not time to turn around and now I was forced to employ the Sten like a club, cracking skull and mashing brain. It was horrible close-quarters work, far grimmer than anything I had ever experienced, but to pause for an instant would mean death from that surging mass of clawing arms, rancid fingers, and rotting teeth. I raised the Sten for another weary swing and my heel gave way, slipping in the ichor and I sank down on one knee before the horde, scrabbling for my pistol to stave off death for a few more precious moments.

Then just as all hope seemed to have departed, a great force pierced the air, a blast of pure, searing energy which danced and rippled through the dead's foetid ranks. It seared and fried them, jumping like chain lightning from each to each, making them twitch and fit like marionettes. It felt as if the very sun itself had flickered in the cave for a moment.

Instinctively, I shielded my eyes from the glare and when it dissipated, the dead fell like their strings had been cut. All that was left, was the smell of dead, roasted, rotting flesh. Without ceremony, I vomited.

"Easy, Major, are you all right?"

"I'm not sure what I am, Seraph, but I'm pretty certain it's a long way from alright. That was you, I take it?"

"Yes, my apologies, I was somewhat preoccupied."

"What was that?"

"A test possibly. It seems we passed."

"Ach, they got Jones, bastards." Sven dabbed at a gash where one of the fallen had raked his face. I wiped the corner of my mouth, got to my feet and spat. The corpses lay piled around us. I was too weary to rage at our latest loss, too tired to do anything more than try and conserve my strength for whatever lay ahead. But something else flickered inside me now too, something important, revenge.

"Well, find him, or whatever's left of him. Take his pack Sven, we'll need it." I heaved my own back onto my shoulders and carefully secured the straps.

"Do you know where von Obertorff is now, Seraph? Can you find him?"

"I believe so, if we—"

"Good, no more questions, just lead the way. Let's go and smoke that bastard out once and for all."

So the final leg of our long journey began, Seraph leading the way like some lanky ethereal hound, while Sven and I followed, eyes and weapons readied. Soon Seraph had found the half-collapsed tunnel mentioned in the journal and as we carefully picked our way down its dark innards, I struggled to concentrate: this mission was meant to thwart the Nazi war effort, but I burned with a desire for vengeance. It is a curious thing to feel such bitter hatred toward someone you have never even met, yet this von Obertorff had much to reckon for. I for one was looking forward to exacting a healthy measure of payment.

The luminescence began to grow in intensity again and then we were on the cusp of the great blasphemous shrine wherein our ultimate foe must surely reside. Sven and I naturally dropped into cover at the entrance, but Seraph continued to walk slowly into the cavern, as if he were taking a casual stroll through Hyde Park.

"No need for concealment gentlemen, he already knows we're here."

Need or not, ingrained military instinct dies hard and there was no value in playing our hand early, so I signalled Sven that we would flank Seraph on either side as we moved into the main body of the cave. In truth, it also helped me focus on more straightforward matters, for this was a disturbing and alien inner vista, which scarcely seemed to belong within the normal realms of our own earth at all. The walls of the great cavern seemed to stretch up beyond the confines of the mountain and out into the stellar void itself, mingling with some terrible alien dimension there. The unnatural light seemed to twist and blend and play tricks with your vision. It was not wholesome to look upon for too long, lest your mind begin to teeter over into the realm of madness.

Yet the cavern itself scarcely proved more settling. There was a dark grove of leafless, blighted trees surrounding the huge central ash like attendant dancers and perhaps it was my imagination, or perhaps not, but they seemed to bend and gyrate slightly as we came forward, as if beckoning us. Now we were close enough to see their abhorrent fruit, a full harvest of bodies, labourers, villagers, even some of the Black Sun, dangling and twisting from their hempen cords. Sven muttered a profoundly filthy curse at the sight of his brother's friends and neighbours hanging there and I believe he was on the point of drawing his hunting knife to go and cut them down, when Seraph's outstretched arm restrained him. So we advanced until we stood before that unholy, evil grove and then Seraph said loudly, "Were you planning on making us wait much longer, von Obertorff?"

For a moment aside the only sound was the sinister, swinging creak of hempen cords. Then came a peal of sardonic laughter, the voice of a man who had fallen into the abyss of madness..

"You British, such sticklers for the correct forms. I believe you would insist on the right teaspoons for dining with the devil himself."

"Perhaps I would, but I don't imagine you'll be passing around the cucumber sandwiches. So, shall we just get to it, von Obertorff? Or perhaps you fear to show yourself in the sight of righteous men?"

"Oh, and now I am disappointed. I had heard you were a man of refinement Herr Seraph, not one for such crude calumnies. Yet, in spite of your rather gauche taunts I will not deny myself the pleasure of making your acquaintance face to face."

From within the folds of the tree trunk emerged a small, sharp featured man, wearing the uniform and greatcoat of an Obergruppen-führer. Despite the imposing uniform and eyepatch, he was a slight individual, difficult to reconcile with the very incarnation of evil which had poured from every word of that terrible journal. That beady eye regarded us with a singular malevolence, which immediately put one on one's guard.

"And you have brought some comrades too. Excellent, my apologies for shall we say 'thinning the herd', but in the wintry fastness of the north, resources are so scarce that every single one must be carefully utilised, I am sure you understand." He waved a gloved hand and now I could see the bodies of Barker, Bennett, and now Jones dangling from a nearby bow. The Sten was at my shoulder in an instant and his face filled my sights, but von Obertorff merely chuckled.

"Bullets won't harm him," said Seraph. "Stand down, Major."

"Very astute, Herr Seraph, for I think you perceive the magnificence of my true form, even if these mortals do not."

"Magnificence is not a word I'd have chosen von Obertorff, though 'abhorrence' might be. Now, let's get to it, why are we here?"

"Why? Because I have chosen to let you."

"Yes, I was rather curious about that. Despite apparently knowing we were coming, you've allowed us to discover your plan, penetrate your defences, enter your inner sanctum and come to the very point of stopping you. It seems a rather questionable strategy."

"Stop me? Ha-ha, very droll, Herr Seraph, but I assure you, you cannot stop me. The truth is I wanted you here, you could even say, I need you to be here." Von Obertorff smiled. "In seeking to free this great weapon, the spear the Norse called Gungnir, but which is in fact a Drottnar artefact of great power as my carefully baited journal no doubt revealed to you – I have expended every soul there was to be had. Untermensch, Aryan, and even the remaining Drottnar hybrids have all been sacrificed to unlock its secret. Behold! "

At this Von Obertorff made a sign with his hand and the trunk of the tree seemed to ripple, the bark peeling in a horribly organic manner to reveal a huge cavity. Inside, suspended in a flaming carapace was a huge, heavy bladed weapon, some eight foot tall and studded with mysterious looking alien sigils and technology.

"Very tragic of course, but it was still not enough. Those ancient witchmen were extremely cunning for so primitive a people and sealed it with powerful magics which have proven remarkably resilient to even my best efforts.

The truth, I have come to realise, is that I could empty a hundred villages, hang a thousand peasants and still not harvest enough magicka, enough soul energy, to release it. So what can I do? Where do I turn? Ah, where else but to the very soul of a witchman himself, or its closest modern equivalent, for that is the richest fuel of all. Even a single one should easily be enough to break down the final barriers.

So, you see, I wanted you to find me, Herr Seraph, I wanted you specifically to find me, because it is only when I have released your soul from the confines of its earthly shell, when I have cracked it open like some scuttling crab and feasted on the soft, juicy pickings inside… it is then, and only then, that I will have enough power to release the Drottnar weapon."

"Never."

"Oh, I think 'never' in this case will be a very short time, Herr Seraph." With that von Obertorff dropped his arms on either side, palms downward and he began to glow with a weird green light. The spear's shrine began to emit small, smouldering, prismatic particles of energy, which streamed out and began spinning around him in elliptical orbits, before being drawn into his body. Under their malign influence he shook, then seemed to swell, grow bigger, more powerful, charged up with each successive impact until it seemed he was almost being consumed by this eldritch force.

Instinctively, Sven and I began to back away from this horrible spectacle, but Seraph held his ground and when von Obertorff seemed swollen almost to the point of bursting, Seraph simply raised his own arms and from his fingertips unleashed bolts of a pure white energy which lanced into the Nazi's green aura, rending the air with a tremendous cascade of sparks. Battle was well and truly joined now and as the two magicians contended, searing bolts of eldritch power raged back and forth, almost obscuring them from sight, as each tested his will against the other. This was no battleground for mortal men, and Sven and I were forced to retreat away from the mystical enfilade, lest we be singed by a stray bolt. Clearly, our bullets would be of little use in a conflict of this kind, yet our true part in the battle was just about to begin.

"Look up there," said Sven pointing to the world tree. "The vizards' fight has summoned it."

Although looking upward into the vault of the cavern made my head swim, I too could see it now, a huge powerful shape swarming from branch to branch, so fast the eye could scarce follow it. Then I lost its path for a moment as it seemed to disappear into the tree itself.

"Major! Look out!" Sven hurled himself into me and we went rolling across the floor of the cavern to fall in a heap. Thank the heavens for Sven's hunter's eyes, for he had seen the beast launch itself off of the main trunk and come hurtling hundreds of feet through the air to land on the exact spot where I had stood. If I had remained there I would have been crushed like an eggshell, but scrambling desperately, we quickly righted ourselves and turned to face our foe.

The Drottnar was a most formidable looking opponent, its colossal nine-foot tall body was powerfully muscled beneath a coat of straggly yellow-white hair, its strapping, brawny arms ended in powerful crushing paws, topped with scimitar-like talons. Its face seemed to combine the most brutish features of wolf and bear, and as its heavy jaw split in a howl of rage, perhaps the most terrifying thing about it of all was the keen, malicious intelligence lurking behind those crimson eyes, as it regarded us, its prey.

For a moment I almost froze and I think it was the raw musky smell emanating from it which transfixed me most, but then instinct took over and my Sten was alive, barking as I emptied a whole magazine into it from its nave to its chops. The bullets left a row of puckered impacts but didn't seem to hurt it visibly and then it extended one of those great paws, talons pointed toward me and pain lacerated my whole right side. I staggered, fell groaning, the Sten dropping uselessly away, looking in disbelief at the spikes of ice which had lodged in my ribs and shoulder.

As I sank to my knees, beyond our immediate struggle, the wizards' duel seemed to be reaching a climax with von Obertorff's malevolent green energies finally threatening to overwhelm Seraph's hard-pressed white. But closer to hand, Sven, perhaps realising the futility of conventional weapons, had drawn ice axe and knife and was advancing on the Drottnar. He was a fierce, brave fellow that man, daring to confront a creature in hand-to-hand combat that could easily rend him limb from limb. But a fierce Viking fire burned in his eyes and as he closed with the beast, he shouted, "Forget the pain, Major and make ready. I will only be able to hold it for so long."

At that I knew what I must do. Throwing off my gloves, I tried to ignore the waves of pain and nausea, and released the straps of the backpack. Sven closed with the Drottnar and it seemed to realise that perhaps here was an opponent worthy of its mettle, for it flexed its great shoulders and snarled at him, a hideous, bestial roar that would have frozen a lesser man's blood.

"Growl *jävel*, I will make you pay for my brother and the villagers!" shouted Sven advancing and with that he sprinted the last few steps and rolled under the Drottnar's raking claws. A backhanded slash of the axe sent a spray of black blood arching through the air and the next moment he had buried the long knife hilt deep into its paw-like foot, causing the creature to bellow with pain and rage. Then he was behind it, darting up its back, grasping its coarse fur like handholds and now he had hold of the back of its head and swung and buried the axe deep into its throat.

For a moment the Drottnar staggered, shaking visibly and I thought he had killed it outright as I fumbled with the valves, but then the great ape-like arms reached up, seized Sven and slammed him into the cavern floor with a sickening retort. The Drottnar reeled, clutching at its wound from which black viscous blood spilled, staining its yellow-white pelt. But then it wrenched out the axe and hurled it away into the depths of the cavern.

Sven, body shattered, groaned and the creature, sensing life in its tormentor yet, lurched across and scooped him up from the cavern floor. Fumbling, I activated the pressuriser and then the igniter sparked, sparked again, and then the hot blue flame lit true. Still clutching one paw to its throat, the Drottnar raised Sven up to eye level with the other, its hand enveloped his whole neck and chest and it held him up there like a child holds a doll. It roared again and was, I believe, about to bite his head clean off in its spite when Sven, head lolling, but summoning the last remnants of strength from his broken body shouted, "Now Major! Now!"

I didn't hesitate. The stream of liquid fire poured out enveloping them both and their screams mingled in an unholy cacophony and the resulting inferno lit up the cavern like a circle of Hades. The beast dropped Sven's burning body and I fired the flamethrower again, emptying every last drop from the tanks, my finger still locked on the trigger long after all the fuel had been expended. The Drottnar writhed and howled and burned until the flames consumed it and all of its filthy life departed and then all that remained was a blackened, empty husk which crumpled to the floor. The smell of burnt fur and petrol was horrendous and dropping the nozzle, I turned and vomited.

The fall of the Drottnar signified a shift in the conflict between Seraph and von Obertorff. Perhaps the loss of his immortal ally weakened von Obertorff somehow, or perhaps their fates were inextricably linked? Who knows? But as I dry-retched the last of my nausea away, it was the Nazi who began to falter.

Now it was Seraph's white corona which expanded and harried and consumed, driving back the waves of pallid green weakening them with every passing second. Yet the force of their cosmic battle was having a marked effect on the cavern too. The great world tree shuddered and groaned, great rocks began to tumble down from the cavernous ceiling and the trees in that cursed grove were disturbed so badly, that many were upturned with their hideous roots exposed, writhing gelatinously in the air. Far above, I could see the very arch of the heavens opened as the two energy streams burst beyond the confines of the cavern and out into the stellar darkness.

The quakes became so violent, the noise so deafening, that I was knocked off my feet and had to scrabble along on all fours or rather on threes: two legs and one arm, the other clutched the aching wounds in my side. Then I heard Seraph's voice, although it may have been nothing more than an illusion bought on by the pain, for it seemed to emanate directly in my mind rather than from any external source. It urged: you can do nothing more, Major. Get out, get out now!

Quickly I looked to Sven's body, but the poor man was far beyond my help and at peace with his ancient gods while the tumult beyond threatened to rend heaven and earth itself. So half blind, half deaf, and half mad with adrenaline and fear, I hopped and scrabbled and dodged and stumbled and fell until somehow I was back at the cavern's entrance. There I stole a last glance inside where Seraph and von Obertorff were still locked in conflict, their magical fire lashing and biting into each other, but Seraph's was stronger now, much stronger, and it was slowly consuming von Obertorff.

Then there was a great crack, like the very firmament itself rupturing, and then the whole cavern was collapsing, tons of rock and dust and debris falling like great hammer blows. Mustering the very last of my reserves, I turned and moved fast as I my wounds would allow, scrambling up the tunnel, desperate to get out of there before I was enveloped by the impending darkness.

That's about as much as I can remember. I awoke a timeless space later in complete darkness and for a long, long while I was simply too weak to do anything but breathe. I lay there wondering if the afterlife consisted of eternal blackness. Yet, whatever its other defining characteristics, I was certain the afterlife wasn't meant to hurt quite this badly and so eventually a lit match from my pocket confirmed that I was still in the tunnel, though the rock fall had sealed off the main cavern.

I still half contemplated just lying there, drifting until eternity swept me away, but the air was bitter and stuffy and I found I had no desire to spend my final moments choking on dust and ashes. My torch was intact and lodging it into my field dress, I supported myself from wall to wall and managed to stumble and lever myself back up the tunnel to the old Viking temple. There I scrounged up some dressings from a fallen body and Jones' rifle made a serviceable crutch to allow me to hobble back towards the surface.

For I knew I was a goner you see. I was too weak to make it down the mountain and even if by some remote chance I managed it, I would simply keel over in the snow on the way back to the village. No, far better to make a more peaceful end of it here at the entrance to the mountain, under the beneficent gaze of the night, where I could smoke a final pipe (I had also retrieved my greatcoat and tobacco naturally) and watch the stars blink out one by one, until I did too.

I relit the bowl and took another deep breath of nicotinous joy. I was sad to think of the deaths of all those brave men I had led, but their sacrifice had not been in vain. It had been a noble fight against a great evil and one that should have echoed and been retold down the centuries. A pity no-one would live to tell this tale and a world would have to make its way without knowing how close it had come to ultimate horror. Perhaps that was for the best after all, perhaps the world was not quite ready for such a revelation?

My one true regret was that I had not been able to thank Seraph for all the help he had given us, his sacrifice in that final battle, and I wished I had had a chance to apologise for all my doubts, petty jealousy and rudeness during the first leg of our mission. That and the fact that there was also no brandy left–which would have been a singular comfort to me at that particular moment, as I contemplated my end.

"Well you know what they say, Major, you should be careful what you wish for, you just might get it. Your apology is accepted," said a voice from the darkness and there, emerging like an angel from the void was Seraph, whole, intact, and apparently uninjured by his recent struggle against that Nazi maniac.

He swung open a German medical kit, (god knows where he had found it), produced a small bottle, knocked off the top and brandished the fiery liquid at me with a knowing smile playing across his curious features. Even though I could not rise to greet him, I could have wept great tears of joy for his return and you know for once, my great British reserve failed me, and I did.

JOIN THE BATTLE AGAINST
THE DEADLY MENACE OF THE MYTHOS!

Delve into the thrilling worlds of the Seraph Chronicles and Mon Dieu Cthulhu! and join Major Seraph and French hussar Gaston Dubois as they begin their fight against the powers of darkness!

Head over to www.john-houlihan.net and sign up for the newsletter to receive a free bonus story from either universe which reveals more about these exciting worlds.

You'll also get updates on new work including the forthcoming Keeper of the Hidden Flame, an epic new adventure in the Mon Dieu Cthulhu! series. In it Gaston Dubois reunites with Major Seraph to be inducted into a secret society who have long guarded humanity against the powers of the dark.

There's also regular freebies, giveaways and competitions and a chance to participate in the development of the forthcoming Mon Dieu Cthulhu! tabletop roleplaying game!

THE SERAPH CHRONICLES
One man defies the might of dread Cthulhu!

The Trellborg Monstrosities

It is 1943 and the war hangs on a knife edge. Set free by a leading Nazi occultist, an ancient evil stirs in the snowy fastnesses of the Norwegian border, threatening to unleash an ancient artefact which could not only alter the course of the war, but the fate of humanity itself.

Hope though endures, as a band of brave resistance fighters and a crack team of British special forces combine to plunge deep behind enemy lines to confront this ancient horror. Yet is their strange civilian adviser, the mysterious Mister Seraph, truly on the side of the angels or pursuing some dark agenda of his own? Can the fearful Trellborg terror even be defeated by mere mortal men?

"A wonderfully evocative tale of blood, bullets and ice." – David J Rodger

The Crystal Void

The year is 1810 and as Napoleon's marshals chase Wellington's expeditionary force through Spain to the lines of Torres Verdras, dashing if rather dim French Hussar Gaston Dubois is astonished to encounter the love of his life.

But the fragrant Odette is abducted before Dubois can consummate his passion by the Marquis Da Foz, a ruthless and sadistic Portuguese nobleman. The hot blooded Hussar is soon in deadly pursuit, but can he evade the Marquis' myriad traps and who is the mysterious ally, Major Seraph, who comes to his aid?

What strange horrors lurk within the shadows of the ancient Moorish fortress where Odette is held captive? Can the heroic duo foil Da Foz's dark machinations, defeat his unnatural allies, rescue Odette and prevent the opening of the dreaded Crystal Void, before it unleashes a new reign of terror on the world?

"Great story, interesting characters, lots of sword and musket action, and the potential for future stories in an underutilised setting."
– Sci-fi and Fantasy Reviewer

Tomb of the Aeons

'The sands of the desert seem as unchanging as the aeons, but they constantly shift reform and remake themselves, so that one is always looking at a frozen moment in perpetual chaos.' – Commander Siegfried

It is 1941 and as Ernst Rommel, the Desert Fox, swings his great armoured right hook to send the British Eighth Army scurrying back toward Egypt, the crew of Ingrid, a mark IV panzer pursue a lone British tank into the deep wastes, only to be ambushed and knocked out.

When they awake, Ingrid's commander Siegfried and his surviving crew begin the long weary trudge back to their own lines, but soon become lost in an unnatural sand storm which seems to blow up from nowhere. When they stumble upon a strange temple complex and find a unit of dead Black Sun SS, they are forced to penetrate deep into the heart of the unholy ziggurat and recover a lost artefact, the Fangs of Set, by their guide and fellow captive Captain Seraph. Will they defeat this charnel house's newly awoken inhabitants and can they survive the horror lurking at the very centre of this tomb of the aeons?

"Indiana Jones meets HP Lovecraft" – Monty Burnham

"The writing is excellent and the atmosphere well-maintained ... it deserves to be widely read." – Sci-fi and Fantasy Reviewer

Before the Flood

The year is 2034 and Britain is a drowning isle, after a cataclysmic wave destroyed her cities, killing millions, raising the sea level by 60 metres and changing the landscape forever.

The Flood has brought Albion to her knees and now the Devils, a race of malevolent sea creatures, haunt her coasts as the survivors retreat inland, struggling for their very existence.

Mankind learns to fear the sea and avoid the water.

Then a mysterious island surfaces off the coast of Wales, a small team of British militia under the command of the war weary veteran Sergeant Emma Stokes, is dispatched to investigate this new threat. But a chance meeting with the mysterious Major Seraph takes them on a dangerous odyssey through this drowned world, to the hidden fortress-city of Gwaelod, which seems to offer new hope in the battle against the creatures. Yet as humanity clutches on by its fingertips, who are the real enemies in this deadly flooded world?

"The shape of water was not a love story, it was a warning."
Amazon Reviewer

"A cracking story. Pick up Before The Flood and devour it, then go onto the rest of the Seraph Chronicles. You'll be in for a hell of a ride!" -
Sci-fi and Fantasy Reviewer

SCIENCE FICTION

The Constellation of Alarion and Other Stories

Best Short Fiction Nominee British Science Fiction Association 2021

Ten insightful science fiction tales from one of British sci-fi and fantasy's most intriguing authors.

John Houlihan is best known for his Cthulhu mythos and historical fantasy series, but this is his first major collection of sci-fi stories, including debut play, Bomber Command.

In Most Exalted, the hero of the seven systems now resides in retirement, but when a series of suspicious deaths rock his veterans' home, will his dubious past finally catch up with him?

In Charioteer, countries settle disputes the old fashioned way, trial by combat. As the eve of a great contest draws close, will Soola finally step out of her brother's shadow and embrace her true destiny?

In the Constellation of Alarion, a fabulous treasure lies hidden in the midst of a deadly labyrinth. Can three galaxy-hopping rogues overcome the maze's lethal traps and their own bumbling inadequacies to claim it?

Explore ten tantalising tales and take a glimpse into a beguiling sci-fi future from one of fantastic fiction's most fascinating talents.

"A masterful collection" Sci-Fi and Fantasy Reviewer

Dark Tales from the Secret War

Dark Tales is a collection of 13 stories set in Modiphius' Achtung! Cthulhu universe, a world which mixes the terrors of HP Lovecraft's Cthulhu mythos with mankind's darkest yet finest hour, the Second World War. Thirteen unhallowed stories await within its covers, which range from the wilds of the South Pacific to the dark depths of the Black Forest, to the icy wastes of Norway. Edited by John Houlihan they come from a stellar cast of writers including David J Rodger, Martin Korda, Richard Dansky and the unsettling mind of horror master Patrick Garratt.

Expanding and exploring the Achtung! Cthulhu universe in bold, new narrative ways, these are the darkest of tales from the Secret War and feature the nefarious Black Sun, Nachtwolfe and their Nazi masters and the heroic Allied forces of Section M and Majestic, as well as many thrilling standalone adventures.

Dark Tales is available from Modiphius.net

MON DIEU CTHULHU!
Swashbuckling supernatural adventure!

The Crystal Void Illustrated Version

The year is 1810 and as Napoleon's marshals chase Wellington's expeditionary force through Spain to the lines of Torres Verdras, dashing if rather dim French Hussar Gaston Dubois is astonished to encounter the love of his life.

But the fragrant Odette is abducted before Dubois can consummate his passion by the Marquis Da Foz, a ruthless and sadistic Portuguese nobleman. The hot blooded Hussar is soon in deadly pursuit, but can he evade the Marquis' myriad traps and who is the mysterious ally, Major Seraph, who comes to his aid?

What strange horrors lurk within the shadows of the ancient Moorish fortress where Odette is held captive? Can the heroic duo foil Da Foz's dark machinations, defeat his unnatural allies, rescue Odette and prevent the opening of the dreaded Crystal Void, before it unleashes a new reign of terror on the world?

"Great story, interesting characters, lots of sword and musket action, and the potential for future stories in an underutilised setting."
— Sci-fi and Fantasy Reviewer

Feast of the Dead

It is late 1810 and as autumn turns to winter, Napoleon's Armee Iberian settles down to its siege of Wellington's "accursed earthworks" at Torres Vedras. Dashing French Lieutenant, Gaston Dubois, is given his first independent command: leading a detachment of hussars those "thieves on horseback" into the Spanish interior, in search of intelligence, supplies and plunder.

After a bloody skirmish, Dubois and his men take refuge at the Monasterio de St Cloud, an ancient ruin standing at the crossroads of this war-torn land, which now serves as a field hospital to soldiers of all nations. There, he encounters the unworldly Doctor Malfeas and the beautiful but fierce Mademoiselle Brockenhurst, who seem to offer temporary respite from the horrors of war.

Yet this former house of the holy holds many strange secrets and Dubois faces fresh battles on all fronts. In his own ranks against the surly Sergeant Sacleaux, his disgraced second-in-command, and externally, by a hostile countryside where every hand is turned against him. Yet most sinister of all is the malevolent mystery which lies at the heart of the Monasterio itself, an ancient and terrible enigma which threatens both the lives and souls of all who encounter it.

Alone, deep behind enemy lines and beset on all sides, will Dubois survive his first real command and can he prevent the horrible unravelling of the mysterious feast of the dead?

"An epic, swashbuckling Napoleonic adventure expertly blended with chilling Lovecraftian horror. One of the most accomplished, entertaining and quietly chilling Horror novels that I've come across in my dive into the genre." – Sci-fi and Fantasy Reviewer

"Highly entertaining, mixing history and fantasy for great adventures ... fall in love with Dubois and his inimitable style." – Egretia.com

Shadow of the Serpent

As the year 1810 wanes, dashing hussar Lieutenant Gaston Dubois finds himself at a crossroads. Following a duel over a crime passionnel, he is banished from his beloved 13th Death's Head Hussars and dispatched in disgrace to the "Accursed" 31st Dragoons

Placed in command of the unruly Second Company in a posting far from the glory and honour he craves, Dubois faces a series of challenges in his first formal command. Can he transform his dispirited men into an effective fighting force, prove his ability to command, and escape the murderous attentions of an odious fellow officer?

But even in this forgotten corner of the war, the forces of mythos and mystery are never far away. Dubois' duel was fought against no mortal man and he is plagued by uncanny events, a countryside hostile to the French occupiers and the wrath of a fearsome guerilla bandita, La Espina, who seems determined to have his head.

Called to arms in a decisive battle against the Spanish army, can Dubois and his company perform in the heat of battle, lead them to victory and restore his reputation and his honour?

www.ingramcontent.com/pod-product-compliance
Lightning Source LLC
Chambersburg PA
CBHW052221150726

48002CB00003B/1219